A Capitalist Carol

The Heroic Tale Of Ebenezer Scrooge
(And That Freeloading Bob Cratchit)

a novel by Ted Satterfield

Copyright © 2018 Ted Satterfield

All rights reserved.

ISBN-13: 9781790445462

Edited by Melanie Wilderman

Cover design by Ted Satterfield

Dedicated to Melanie.

The comfort, encouragement, and advice were all great, but this dedication is specifically for not slugging me every time I asked, "Hey, does this sentence sounds stupid?", which was like a billion times.

But, seriously, this never would have happened without you. You helped me see that this idea was worth pursuing. Writing a book is never easy, but writing a weird book is a bonkers, batshit nightmare. You were with me the whole way. I'll never forget that.

THANKS!

A SPECIAL THANKS to Stacey, Jennifer, and another Jennifer. First off, all three of you laugh at my jokes, which is reason enough for me to like you. But wait, there's more: Two of you are amazing friends, who were kind enough to read my drafts, and provide me with valuable feedback. Both of you had remarkable critiques and insights, and I'll forever be grateful for the blind spots you helped me see. The other Jennifer helped in ways far beyond the scope of this book, and since certain fields can be down-right-fucking thankless, I want to take this unique opportunity to say, "Thank you!!!!"

Attention grammar nerds!

A **SPECIAL NOTE** to those who still give a shit about grammar, punctuation, and spelling. I should warn you that I use some unusual punctuation in the upcoming text, notably, at times, you'll see commas used with a coordinating conjunction before a dependent clause. I understand this is blasphemy for punctuation zealots, like me, but people with visual impairments are often reliant on assistive technologies, such as screen-readers and text-to-voice software, which do not add pauses a sighted reader might naturally infer. I had this in mind during my placement of all punctuation, capitalization, and use of homonyms. Please continue to give a cornucopia of shits about the above mentioned rules, and allow me to tailor this text to be as friendly to visually-impaired readers as I can.

And for those of you who plan to use text-to-voice on this book, I sincerely hope you appreciate hearing computers say words, such as shit, fuck, dick, ass, and tits, as much as me.

Enjoy!

A CAPITALIST CAROL

The <u>heroic</u> tale of Ebenezer Scrooge and that <u>free-loading</u> Bob Cratchit

By Ted Satterfield

CHAPTER 1: MARLEY'S GHOST
or
MUSINGS ABOUT MY DEAD BUSINESS PARTNER

Let's get something out of the way first: Marley was dead. No doubt! I should know. Since he had no family, or friends, I got stuck making all the burial arrangements. I got stuck signing all the burial papers. I also had to watch them lower his wrinkled, old corpse into the grave.

Yep! Old Marley was stone-fucking dead.

***

Dickens stopped typing, as he questioned whether that last line went too far. He knew the word "fuck" was vulgar, but he wasn't sure exactly HOW vulgar. The last few days, Dickens absorbed plenty about 21st Century America, but he still had knowledge gaps — cavernous knowledge gaps — having spent his Birth Life in 19th-Century England.

The Revision software on his computer was no help on this matter. It displayed a box to the left of the screen, filled with the original text of "A Christmas Carol." To the right, sat an empty box for him to type the Revised version. Currently, a cursor blinked inside the box after the words, "stone-fucking dead," taunting him with every blink.

He perused the reference books shelved at his cubicle, hoping one of them would offer vulgarity guidelines. First on the top shelf sat an N.I.V. Bible, which likely wouldn't answer questions about modern vulgarity. He wanted to figure out what "N.I.V." meant, but fighting the temptation to get sidetracked, he moved on. Scanning the shelf, left to right, he read the reference book titles:

King James Bible

New King James Bible

New American Standard Bible

New Texas Standard Bible

The Electrifying Bible (Aggressive Translation)

The On-Fire-For-Jesus Bible (Teen Edition)

'Victorian English' to 'Modern American English' Dictionary

Literary Revision Room Style Manual

Dictionary of American Clichés

A dictionary, simply titled "Dictionary"

A book called "He's Coming Back Soon" (50th Anniversary Edition)

And, finally, three books that looked to be a series, titled "God's Prosperity Promise," "Blessed or Oppressed?" and "Poor No More!!!"

It didn't seem as if any of those books would help. Leaning back in his chair, he contemplated the situation. His head hanging slightly outside the walls of his cubicle, he scanned the room. The cubicles were grouped in clusters of four, but the tall partitions blocked his view from seeing any other Revisers.

The cubicles were gray. The desks were gray. The carpet was gray. The walls were gray. The fluorescent lights on the ceiling were framed with metal, also gray.

Pretty typical for a 21st-Century office complex, with one exception: Every entrance to the room was flanked by guards holding high-caliber rifles.

The guards all looked the same. If not for the numbers stitched on their lapels, they were indistinguishable. Appearing to have never laughed in their lives, they maintained hyper-intense expressions, as if engaged in a life-or-death staring contest. They were all under 30 years old and suited up as if anticipating an ambush. A little excessive, since Revisers were not only unarmed, but also much older. Dickens, having died at 58, and, therefore, Resurrected at 58, was among the youngest.

With his head tilted outside his cubicle, Dickens saw a guard glaring at him. Whipping his head back, his fake mustache flew off and landed on the keyboard. He looked down to grab it, causing his hairpiece to fall off, too. Using the faint reflection in the monitor, he attempted to get them back on straight.

They were straight, but he looked ridiculous, like a man in a Charles Dickens costume. Wearing fake hair was mandatory, assuming you had hair in your Birth Life. It was allegedly fashioned from a photograph of him, but he wondered which photograph, and whether it was really him.

Like all Revisers, Dickens wore a gray-and-white-striped prison jumpsuit with the initials CRC on the back. The suit made his fake mustache and wig look even sillier, even more like a man on his way to a costume party. The reasoning behind the hair, as explained during The Orientation: "You'll feel more like yourself while you write." It might have made sense if Revisers weren't forced to remove the hair when returning to their evening quarters. He could look like himself when he couldn't see himself, but, in the evening, all he'd see is a shaved head and face.

He turned his head, slowly this time, to check if the guard was still glaring. He was. Dickens spun back to his computer, accepting that, in this environment, he didn't have the luxury of peaceful contemplation about his writing. He needed to make a quick decision. He REALLY liked the sound of the phrase "Stone-Fucking Dead," so he kept it, and moved on with his writing.

***

… Old Marley was stone-fucking dead.

Mind you, stones aren't any deader than other inanimate objects, regardless of their igneous or sedimentary status, but, for the sake of brevity, let me repeat, emphatically: MARLEY WAS STONE-FUCKING DEAD.

Did I, Ebenezer Scrooge, know it? Of course. He was my partner — in the business sense, not the "gay" sense — for many years. I was his only associate, his only colleague, and the only person who could fucking stand him. Though I was not particularly whimpery about his demise, I am a terrific businessman. Even on the day of the funeral, I found a way to capitalize on that old fart's death.

At the risk of becoming absurdly redundant, I will repeat that there is zero doubt whether Marley was dead. No coma. No Code-Blue-but-we-might-zap-him-back-to-life-with-defibrillators BULLSHIT — that old bitch was dead.

If you don't understand that point, the rest of this story won't make sense. I'm not trying to pull one of those cornball twists where you didn't expect him to be a ghost, since, "He was dead the whole time."

***

Dickens questioned whether it was too obvious "He was dead the whole time" referred to the movie "The Sixth Sense." The film was fresh in his mind, having only watched it yesterday, but the films he was forced to watch were apparently popular. He was supposed to avoid changes to his book that could reveal this was a Revised version of the original. Since "The Sixth Sense" was released 150 years AFTER "A Christmas Carol," a discerning reader might suspect something was off.

He liked the line, though, and decided to leave it in. If he got in trouble, he could plead ignorance. Ignorance was a valid excuse. In the absurdity of this Revision task, it should be expected. Besides, it was his first day on the job. Doesn't everybody get a little leeway on their first day?

Turning his attention back to his writing, he decided to force Ebenezer Scrooge to stop rambling.

***

I should stop rambling and get to the point: Despite his death, I never removed Marley's name. Seven years later, the sign still stood above the door: Scrooge and Marley. The firm was known as "Scrooge and Marley," but snarky fuckers liked to call it, "Scrooge, Scrooge, and sometimes Marley." All the same to me.

Marley's name was good for business. In my worldview, if it's good for business, it's good.

***

Dickens stopped in a fit of frustration. His index fingers cramped from two-fingered typing, which he tried to relieve with finger stretches, as if gesturing single air quotes. Plus, hunting and pecking the words on the keyboard took 10-times longer than a pen. His captors might not care about discomfort, but surely, they'd care about the speed of his progress. He decided to ask if there was ANY flexibility.

He raised his hand to flag down his boss, prompting suspicion from all four guards assigned to Dickens. The Supervisor didn't notice, lost in his own world watching two men fighting in a cage on television. He started to wave his hand frantically, which forced one of his guards, with "Guard 93" on his lapel, to walk over to The Supervisor's desk. He nodded to the guard, stood up, and, annoyed at the interruption of his TV show, walked over to Dickens' cubicle.

"What's wrong?" The Supervisor said in a thick, Texas accent.

Dickens didn't think he'd heard a Texas accent on his trips to America during his Birth Life. But, at the moment, his memory was understandably fuzzy.

"Well, sir," Dickens said, in a tone he hoped came across as genuine, not whiny. "I am wondering if this is necessary."

The Supervisor rolled his eyes, twanging out, "It's extremely necessary you Revise this book."

"I understand Revising my novella is necessary," Dickens said, pointing toward his computer. "But must I use this machine?"

Puzzled, The Supervisor asked, "Are you wantin' one of them Apples?"

Dickens had no idea what fruit had to do with anything, but he let it go.

"Sir," he said, almost pleading. "May I use a pen? I could work significantly faster."

"Ohhhhhh," he said with a comedically-slow drawl. "I see what you mean. We need it done on a computer. The software was built in-house specifically for Revisions. Plus, the Revision Oversight Team tracks your progress."

Dickens returned a look of concern.

"You know?" he said, pointing up in the air. "Up in the cloud or whatever."

Dickens thought to himself: Apple? Cloud? What on earth is this dimwit talking about?

He took a deep breath, and said, "Very well. We mustn't do anything to disrupt the cloud. In time, I'm sure I'll grow accustomed to this machine."

"You will," The Supervisor said. "My daddy refused to touch a computer until they put NASCAR online, but now, he's addicted. It'll take you a while, but once you get used to it, you'll think you've died and gone to heaven."

"Of course," Dickens said, disappointed. "Thank you."

"Sure thing," The Supervisor said, slapping him on the back a little too hard.

Dickens turned back to his computer as The Supervisor walked back to his television.

Under his breath, Dickens forcefully said, "I. Did. Die."

He proceeded with his two-fingered typing. Hammering the keyboard with each letter, writing in the first person of Ebenezer Scrooge.

***

I've been called a lot in my days.

"Old, Scrooge," they'd say, "is a cheap bastard, always screwing over the little guy. He's a lonely, old hermit, who only emerges from the shadows for a chance to screw over someone else."

They act as if that's a bad thing.

"He's an ugly old piece of shit," they say. "Can't get a woman, even though he's rich."

Well, that's fine with me. Diamonds are, apparently, a woman's best friend. Diamonds cost money. I'll let some other sap spend his money on that noise.

Women are whack. But, money, is the bomb. It's all that and a bag of chips.

***

Dickens stopped typing.

"All that and a bag of chips?" he repeated, slowly, to himself. "What in hell does that mean?"

He'd found these phrases in the reference book: "Common American Clichés." He was instructed to insert modern clichés into his Revisions whenever possible. The thought made him want to gag, but what could he do? They had guns. He didn't.

During The Orientation, he was urged to Revise using current American vernacular. Americans, apparently, were the target audience. He'd picked up loads of modern terms and phrases, being forced to watch modern movies and television Clockwork Orange-style. The reference books were supposed to fill in any remaining gaps.

One member of the Department of Literary Revision told him, "We want to get rid of that fruity Englishman talk." The man told Dickens he didn't even mind if some cursing were added, if it didn't "go too far," and didn't sound like "Pansy British cussin'."

Adding curse words was the lone bright spot about the Revision, since Dickens had formed an affinity for the modern word "fuck." A term he'd, obviously, heard before, but in his day, it was a crass term for sexual intercourse. Now it was suitable in infinite contexts. It could be funny. Foul. Frightful.

It proved deeply satisfying to write or say. A one syllable word, initiated with an "F," elegantly suspended with an "UH," and slammed shut with a hard "K". Phonetically powerful, but somehow still a pleasant note in our verbal symphony.

"Fuck!" Dickens said to himself during The Orientation. "I'm going to use that word every fucking chance I get."

With his love of the word making him feel warm inside, he returned to the description of Scrooge's love of money:

***

People think I'm cold as fuck. I'm okay with that. I never understood humans who get all warm and squishy about other humans. Especially at Christmas. The stupidest time of the year, where all the saps get extra sappy.

I make my way along the crowded paths of life, warning all humans to keep their distance. Even blind people's dogs steer their masters away from me. Dogs are smarter than humans. They know up which tree they should not bark.

But, I'll get to my point. This story begins on Christmas Eve, as I sat at my desk at work. It was an exceptionally cold winter's day, when annoying fuckers dress up like they're on an arctic expedition, and THEN feel the need to ask, "Is it cold enough for ya?"

The clocks had just struck three, but it was completely dark. It hadn't been "light" at any point of the "day," as the morning fog hung around like an unwelcome houseguest.

The business I owned was a counting house.

***

Dickens grabbed the "'Victorian English' to 'Modern American English' Dictionary," to see how best to describe a counting house to his modern readers. He found no information on counting houses. He tried the generic dictionary. There was nothing in that either, but he did read a few entries in the "C.o.u."

section. There was a fascinating entry on "Country Western Music" and a baffling one on something called "Count Chocula".

Realizing the books were no help, he tried to construct his own definition of a counting house. If his cloudy memory was correct, they served a variety of needs, and differed greatly from one counting house to another. If he was confused about it himself, certainly his readers would also be confused.

This confusion gave him a spectacular idea for how to proceed with the writing:

**

What is a "counting house?" you might ask. It doesn't matter. We moved money around in one way or another. Loaned a little. Tracked a little. Counted a lot. The takeaway here is this: We didn't make anything, but we still raked in cash.

People think making money requires "building things" or "creating stuff." That's a waste of time. Making junk only gets in the way.

If you want to build something, build it. If you want to make money, make it. Anyone who thinks the former is required to generate the latter, is a sucker. If that hurts your feelings, stop reading.

Seriously, if it does, stop!

If you're expecting a change of heart for old Ebenezer Scrooge, I'll save you the suspense. If you want a greedy man to see the error of his ways, you've picked up the wrong fucking book.

Want a change of heart? Go watch "Pretty Woman."

**

Dickens knew he'd have to scratch that last line the second he typed it. He watched "Pretty Woman" during The Orientation, and he rather liked it. In it, the greedy man learns, from a wise and kind-hearted harlot, that he's a worthless asshole. It ends with him changing his ways, much like Scrooge in his original book. Sadly, in this Revision, Ebenezer would be just as greedy on the last page as he was on the first.

Scrooge would learn no lesson in this tale. There was nothing for him to learn. The reader was to learn from him. The mean, selfish, evil man would show them how they ought to live. This was the whole reason he'd been Resurrected: to transform "A Christmas Carol" into a book friendlier to Capitalism, for use in American schools.

Readers, especially schoolchildren, would be right to expect that the mean man wouldn't win in the end. They could be crushed with this new ending. He had no choice but to make the changes, but, hopefully, this "Don't Expect a Change of Heart" disclaimer would kill expectations of a morally-satisfying ending. Maybe they'd stop reading altogether. At the moment, this was his best scheme.

Catching a nasty glare from Guard 94, he knew he'd need to resume typing soon. He was oddly grateful for the glare. It would keep him working, which might keep him from ruminating about his unpleasant situation, which might keep him sane. He forced his mind to snap back to the Revision.

The "Pretty Woman" reference would get scrapped. He was confident the vague-ish reference to "The Sixth Sense" would be fine, but, even though he'd been less-than-impressed with the intellect of his captors, a direct reference to a movie from the 1990s wouldn't slip past even the stupidest of humans. He deleted it.

**

~~Want a change of heart? Go watch "Pretty Woman."~~

Seriously, no change of heart is coming.

I was sitting in my office with the door open to keep an eye on my clerk, Bob Cratchit. The fire next to his desk was burning out, badly in need of more coal. The pitiful bastard was obviously freezing, hovering his hands above a candle for warmth.

It's not my fault he's too poor to buy his own coal, and it's not fair for him to get any of mine. I've NEVER bought coal. I've been saving coal since I was a kid. My father would give it to me in my stocking at Christmas, supposedly as punishment for being "bad." It makes no sense, coal being such an efficient source of energy. My clerk was probably a "good" kid who got worthless toys at Christmas, but now look at him. A grown man looking for a handout to keep himself from freezing.

If he's such a pussy when it's cold, maybe he shouldn't have had all those damn kids. If he'd kept all the money he'd wasted feeding those little parasites, he could buy heaps of coal.

***

Dickens stopped typing. During The Orientation, he was warned against making negative references to the oil, gas, and coal industries. What those industries entailed, he didn't know. Nor did he know why they needed protection against Christmas-themed novellas.

"Do modern children WANT coal in their stockings at Christmas?" Dickens mumbled to himself.

"I'd keep writing if I were you," said a man with a thick German accent on the other side of his cubicle.

Dickens tried standing just enough to see the German man, but as soon as he lifted up from his chair, security guards surrounded him, guns drawn. An alarm started blaring, as The Supervisor rushed out of the room. The other Revisers slowly raised their hands, their fingers barely peaking over the tops of their cubicles. Dickens wasn't given instructions on what to do next, leaving him frozen in a half-standing, half-squatting stance. He fought to keep his trembling to a minimum.

The Supervisor ran back in, alongside a stern-looking young man who made Dickens feel uneasy. As he approached the cubicle, his stare could have lit a fire.

"What is all this, 84?" the man said, directing his attention to a guard.

"Mr. Overseer, sir!" Guard 84 said. "Dickens stood up during Designated Revision Time."

The Overseer stood silently, still staring daggers. After an uncomfortable moment, the man's face softened a little, as he said, "stand down, men. Good job!"

The guards lowered their weapons and walked back to their posts. The Overseer moved closer to Dickens, who remained uncomfortably half-crouched.

"You can have a seat," he said to Dickens. Turning his head toward The Supervisor, he said, "You go have a seat, too."

The Supervisor lowered his head in shame, walking back to his desk. Dickens, his hands still raised, slowly sat down.

"Lower your hands," The Overseer said to him, after which, he yelled to the rest of the room, "Y'all lower your hands, too. I wanna hear a whole lot of typin'!"

Dickens lowered his hands while all of the keyboards in the room resumed their clattering.

The Overseer leaned up against his desk and folded his arms.

"Well, well, well," he said. "It's the magnificent Charles Dickens."

"Yes," Dickens said, still shaken. "I wanted to stretch my legs. I wasn't trying to …"

"My father is a huge fan of your work," he interrupted, with a grin. "I don't get it, but he thinks you're really something special."

"Oh," Dickens said, unsure whether to respond as insulted or complimented. "That's great."

"I hope he gets a chance to meet you," The Overseer said, dropping the grin. "But you ain't shit to me."

Dickens tried to swallow, but his mouth was too dry.

"So, the next time you decide to stretch your legs," The Overseer said. "I'll have them broken."

"Yes, sir," Dickens said.

"Good boy," The Overseer said, patting his head as a child would a puppy. "Now get back to work. I need to go have a chat with your Supervisor."

He walked over to The Supervisor's desk, whispered something to him, and the two men walked out of the Revision Room.

Dickens watched the door, trying to overhear their conversation. A squeaking sound across the room distracted him. A man in his 50s approached Guard 93, rolling a desk chair with noisy wheels. The guard examined the chair from top to bottom, and motioned for the man to follow.

"Mr. Dickens," Guard 93 said. "I need you to stand up."

He stood up and stepped to the side. The man, "Custodian 8" stitched on his shirt, pulled out Dickens' chair and exchanged it for the squeaky one. The custodian folded up a towel and placed it in the seat of the chair. He was confused about what was happening, until he noticed the smell. At some point in the excitement, he had pissed himself. A wave of schoolboy-like embarrassment swept over him. He felt his face grow red.

"You can take a seat again, Dickens," Guard 93 said. "And get back to writing."

The guard resumed his post along the doorway, while Custodian 8 rolled the urine-soaked chair out of the Revision Room. He tried to compose himself enough to continue Revising, but his hands were shaking, and the smell of urine stung his eyes.

"Keep writing," the German voice said, much quieter than before. "And never stand up."

"I gathered that," Dickens said, whispering back. "Fuck!"

"You don't want to end up like Charles," the German man said.

"Charles?" he asked.

"Not you," the man said. "Darwin."

"Charles Darwin is here?" he asked.

"They moved him to another sector," the man said, gloomily. "For punishment."

"Really?"

"Yes," the German man said. "Ironically, Darwin was not fit to survive."

Dickens began to laugh but caught himself before he made a sound. Knowing eyes were watching him closer than ever, and since his trembling had eased enough to resume typing, he swung his attention back to Revising. There was no time to wait around for inspiration, and since the one fragment of inspiration he had revolved around the word "fuck," he attacked the page, aiming to use it as frequently as possible.

***

Cratchit could bring his own fucking coal.

"A merry Christmas, uncle!" said a chipper-as-fuck voice. "God save you!"

The voice was that of my pain-in-the-ass nephew, who was prone to popping into my office with the subtlety of a jack in the box.

The sight of him sickened me, and the only response I could muster was, "Bah! Go fuck yourself!"

***

Dickens had typed "Bah! Go fuck yourself!" fully aware it wasn't a suitable replacement for "Bah! Humbug!" But, it was the phrase bubbling up within him, so, he went with it.

***

"Christmas a humbug, uncle?" my nephew said. "You don't mean that."

"Humbug?" I asked. "I said go fuck yourself."

"Surely, you don't mean that either," he said.

"I do, you little shit!" I said. "Why on earth would YOU be merry? You're poor as fuck."

"Uncle, you have more money than you could spend in a lifetime," my fruity nephew said. "What right have you to be angry?"

Struggling to think of a fitting response, I said "Bah!" and followed it up with a forceful "Go fuck yourself!"

"Oh, be nice," said my dandy-pants nephew.

"Nice?" I asked, "when I live in a world of pathetic, freeloading losers? Merry Christmas? What's Christmas but an excuse for moochers to spend money they don't have, racking up debt they could never pay off. Come January, they'll all be looking for people … LIKE ME … to bail them out. If it were up to me, every dumbass floating around, flogging people with Merry Christmases, would have a candy cane thrust through his heart …

"Oh, uncle?" my nephew interrupted.

" … and be boiled in a vat of figgy pudding!" I said with the conviction of a preacher.

"Uncle," my nephew repeated.

"Nephew!" I returned. "Observe Christmas in your own way, and let me observe it in mine."

"Observe it?" He said. "You don't observe it."

"That's my point, you sniveling FART KNOB!" I said. "It's never done me any good. It's never done ANYONE any good!"

"Good is what Christmas is all about," my foppish nephew said. "It's the only time of the year when men and women thaw their frozen hearts, thinking of people less fortunate as brothers and sisters on our inevitable voyage to the grave. So, uncle, Christmas has never done anything to make me richer, but it has done me good, and will do me good. And I say, 'God bless it!'"

Before I could respond, my dip-shit clerk leapt to his feet and applauded.

"One more outburst from you," I said, pointing at Cratchit, "and I'll throw you out on your holly-jolly ass."

"And you," I said, turning back to my nephew. "Since you're so good at delivering speeches laced with delusional optimism, you should go into politics."

"Oh, don't get angry," my nephew said. "Come have dinner with us tomorrow."

"You can take your Christmas dinner," I said, "and shove it up Rudolph's ass!"

"But why?" my nephew said, in a whinier voice than before. "Why are you acting like this?"

"Please leave," I said, bluntly.

"We're family," he said. "Can't we act like family once a year?"

"Get out!" I yelled.

"Very well, uncle," he said, "But I'm not going to let YOUR negativity dampen MY Christmas spirit. So, I'll say it again: A Merry Christmas, uncle!"

"Rot in hell!" I said.

"And A Happy New Year!" my nephew said.

"Go strait to hell!" I said.

***

After Dickens typed this line, he noticed on his computer screen a small, yellow frowning face form at the end of the word "hell," almost as if indicating a footnote.

"Hey," Dickens whispered through the cubicle to the German man. "What does it mean if a word gets a little unhappy face next to it?"

"The software is flagging something you wrote," he said. "The program alerts us to various things Revision Oversight would not like. What did you say?"

"I said 'Go strait to hell.'"

The German man laughed quietly, and said, "You can't say that."

"Why not?"

"Mr. Dickens, you are in 21st-Century America," he said. "In fact, you're in the American state of Texas. They're a bit touchy about religion."

"Oh," he said. "I hadn't been briefed about that."

"Well," he said, "you can take my word for that, Mr. Dickens."

"Charles," he said, a tad awkwardly. "You can call me Charles if you'd like."

"OK, Charles." the man said. "It's nice to meet you. I'd stand up, but I don't want to get shot."

Dickens laughed.

"You may call me, Friedrich."

"Nietzsche?" he asked. "I remember reading about you."

Friedrich laughed again, saying, "That's the first time I've heard my name pronounced correctly since my Birth Life."

"Seriously?"

"Neee-Cheee," Friedrich said, mimicking a Texas accent. "That's how these Texans say it. Neee! Cheee!"

Dickens laughed a little too hard at this. He caught a stern glance from The Supervisor, who had reentered the room without him noticing. He abruptly stopped laughing, and directed his attention back to his computer screen.

Dickens looked at his previous line, where he wrote, "Go strait to hell!". He noticed, even though "hell" was spelled correctly, he had used "strait" instead of "straight". He grabbed the dictionary and looked up the words "strait" and "straight," and sure enough, the spelling hadn't changed.

How odd, he thought, that this program was sophisticated enough to identify undesirable religious references, but a misspelled word went undetected.

He wanted to bring this subject up to Nietzsche, whom he knew would have a hilarious quip about the bizarre linguistic priorities, but when he opened his mouth to say something, he saw The Supervisor looking at him like an angry schoolmaster. Like an ill-behaved schoolboy who'd been caught in the act, Dickens lowered his head and returned to his writing.

***

My nephew smiled with a big dumb grin, turned and walked toward the door, clearly still in a terrific mood. He tipped his hat to my worthless clerk who smiled and waved.

"There's another fellow," I said to my nephew, but well aware my clerk could hear it. "My clerk, with fifteen shillings a week, and a wife and family, talking about a Merry Christmas."

My nephew and my clerk both pretended not to hear me, as the clerk stood up to open the door for my nephew, but in doing so, carelessly let in two other people.

Two fat-ass men waddled in, removed their hats, and stood inside the door holding clipboards stacked with paper. They bowed toward me.

"Scrooge and Marley's, I believe," said one of the fat asses, as he looked down at his clipboard. "To whom am I now speaking, Mr. Scrooge, or Mr. Marley?"

"Mr. Marley died seven years ago," I said, hoping he'd feel like a jerk for asking. "On this very night."

"We have no doubt he was a generous man who is sorely missed," Fat Ass #1 said with a chipper tone, proving I had not made them feel like jerks.

He handed me his credentials, which I didn't even pretend to look at before I handed them back.

"At this festive season of the year, Mr. Scrooge," Fat Ass #2 said, taking up a pen, "Most of us take our eyes off ourselves and turn them toward the poor and destitute.

Thousands don't have enough to eat, and hundreds of thousands lack adequate clothing for the bitterness of winter."

"Are there no prisons?" I asked.

"Plenty of prisons," said Fat Ass #1 with confusion, laying down the pen again.

"What about workhouses?" I asked.

***

Dickens stopped typing, as he thought to himself: "I hope there are no workhouses anymore." But the mere fact he was being asked to make his book less sympathetic to the poor, didn't bode well for his hopes of poor people getting treated with dignity. The thought saddened him greatly, but he tried to push this out of his mind as he continued typing.

***

"Workhouses are open and still as soul-crushing as ever," Fat Ass #2 said.

"Oh, I'm glad to hear that," I said. "The taxes are ripped out of my pockets to pay for that nonsense. I was concerned my tax dollars were being earmarked for things even more useless."

The fat asses gave one another a puzzled look and went back to their pathetic pitch.

"Since the need is so great, we are raising funds for food and clothing," Fat Ass #1 said. "We chose this time of the year, as we all, no doubt, look at our positions of privilege and take notice of those less fortunate."

"Privilege?" I said with disgust.

"Yes, sir. Privilege," Fat Ass #1 said, clueless that the suggestion of privilege disgusted me. "What should I put you down for?"

"Nothing!" I said, abruptly.

"I see," Fat Ass #2 said. "You wish to be anonymous?"

"I wish to be left alone," I said. "Since you ask me what I wish, gentlemen, that is my answer. I am not a fortunate man. I am not a 'privileged' man."

I flashed two sarcastic air quotes as I said the word "Privileged."

"I EARNED every cent I've ever made," I said. "I am responsible with every one of those cents not ripped out of my pockets for taxes. And since I am responsible with MY money, I see no value in taking more of those cents out of MY pockets so a bunch of freeloaders can be 'Merry'."

I flashed another set of sarcastic air quotes as I said the word "Merry."

"But without these necessities, people will die," Fat Ass #2 said.

"That's a good point," I said, and paused for a moment of contemplation. With a smile, I continued with, "If they die, that could make a substantial dent in the surplus population."

"Sir, have you no heart?" Fat Ass #1 said.

"Of course," I said, "one's circulatory system isn't much use without a heart."

"No, I mean, how can you say such a thing?" Fat Ass #1 said.

"It's easy," I said, standing to show my patience had worn thin. "It's not MY business!"

The two fat asses were stunned.

I continued, saying, "it's enough for a man to understand his own business. My business takes up all of my time, and I do not wish to waste it anymore. So, get the fuck out!"

With this, the two fat asses finally realized it was a lost cause, so they lowered their heads, turned, and walked out.

***

Having found a rhythm for the first time since he began his Revisions, Dickens failed to notice most words he'd written in this last section bore little yellow faces. But, his time, the faces were happy.

"Hey," Dickens whispered through the cubicle. "Friedrich?"

"Yes, Charles?" he asked.

"I'm getting those faces again," he said. "They're on most words of an entire scene."

"Happy? Sad? Concerned?" Nietzsche asked.

"Well," he said, "they look happy to me."

Nietzsche let out a one syllable laugh.

"Is that not a good sign?" Dickens asked.

"'GOOD' is a relative concept," Nietzsche said. "But, whatever you're writing, the Revision Oversight Team LOVES."

"That's disappointing," he said. "I was hoping I'd gone too far."

Scrooge wasn't a subtle character to begin with, but sadly, Dickens' view of over-the-top greedy and self-centered, was ideal to his captors. Objectively, not GOOD.

Looking a little gloomier than before, he returned to his writing.

***

When it was closing time at the counting house, my always-eager-to-leave clerk quickly blew out his candle and put on his hat.

"Let me guess," I said. "You want off all fucking day tomorrow?"

Sheepishly, my clerk said, "If that's convenient for you, sir."

"It's not convenient," I yelled, "and it's not fair. If I docked your salary for missing tomorrow, you'd whine like a little bitch, wouldn't you?"

Bob maintained a weak smile.

"And yet," I said, "I have to bend over and take it up the ass, so you can fart around with your family."

The clerk's smile grew fainter.

"YOU chose to have a family," I said. "Yet, I'M the one punished."

Bob looked uncomfortable, which amused me, so I continued.

"It's a bullshit excuse for picking a man's pocket every 25th of December!" I said, putting on my coat. "You better be here early as fuck on the 26th."

"Oh, I will, sir," the clerk said. "Thank you, sir."

I locked up, and we went in our separate ways, but the clerk, very irritatingly, stopped and yelled, "Merry Christmas, Mr. Scrooge!"

I turned halfway around, and fired back with, "Bah, go fuck yourself!"

***

A window appeared on Dickens' computer. It stated, in bright-red letters: "Caution! You are nearing your limit on curse words!" He opened his mouth to ask Nietzsche's advice, but it was self-explanatory.

Deflated, he shut his eyes and muttered, "Fuck!"

***

Getting the last word with my nephew, the fat-asses, and Bob Cratchit, made my walk from work delightful. I gleefully skipped to my typical cheap-ass tavern, devoured my typical cheap-ass dinner, and frolicked home.

I lived in an apartment building my deceased partner once owned. It would have cost a fortune to repair the decomposing structure, far more than I could recoup from renters. Therefore, I lived there alone. I did find a few saps willing to rent rooms as artist studios, appreciating how the place was shabby as fuck.

***

"Fuck!" Dickens whisper-yelled.

He questioned whether he had the discipline to stop using the word "fuck." Despite the warning, he didn't write a hundred words before mindlessly typing it. It was frustrating, knowing there was a limit, but only knowing he was "nearing" it. Was it the number of "fucks" per page? One "fuck" per thousand words? Could he use "fuck" to his heart's content if he avoided other curse words?

Perhaps the vagueness could work to his advantage? The warning didn't say: "stop typing 'fuck'." After all, vulgarity is cultural. He could claim, in his Birth Life, "Figgy" meant lumpy and "Pudding" meant feces. Or Bob meant "sticky" and "Cratchit" meant ejaculate. If he thought the alert was because of those words, would they do the research to prove him wrong?

Those held captive must cling to something. Sure, normally it's love for someone, or hope for the future, but, survival is survival. If he stood up, he would get shot, but, to survive, he needed to stand up for something. His love for the word "fuck" would have to do.

He decided to risk it, and, out of love for the word, and defiance to his captors — and their fucking software — he inserted a pointless chapter and wrote "fuck" twice in the heading.

CHAPTER 1½: MARLEY'S FUCKING GHOST

or
I SWEAR A FUCKING GHOST WILL APPEAR SOON

The outer door to my building had a door knocker. Many of you are, understandably, thinking, "No fucking shit!" Please trust that your straight-forward narrator would not dwell on this if it wasn't important. The knocker wasn't special. It wasn't fancy or memorable, even to me, who saw it every fucking day.

So, having made all that shit clear, when I slid my key in the lock, the knocker transformed into the face of my stone-fucking dead business partner, Jacob Marley. As I leaned in to look closer at the phenomenon, it was instantly a knocker again.

The level of fright was a tad beyond "feeling goosebumps," but not quite to "shitting my pants." I closed the door behind me, and, for a second, felt compelled to turn around to see the opposite side of the door. I halfway expected to see the back of Marley's head poking through. But I saw nothing. Just a door. Nothing special about it either.

***

Dickens stopped typing, experiencing a peculiar sensation of déjà vu. Not of an event, but of a feeling. He noticed it when he first stepped into the Revision Room, but he was unable to isolate the exact feeling. Grief, frustration, and helplessness had masked the scent of this déjà vu, but, suddenly, he knew what it was:

Empathy, as he experienced visiting his father in debtors' prison. A feeling of empathy for those who suffered in that dreadful place. Empathy not bound to the present. It reached back in time, sensing the suffering of former captives. Suffering that lingered like the stale air of a motel room, constantly reminding you of the strangers who'd once made this space their home. Empathy that attached itself to you. Became part of you. Urged you to help stop future suffering; the only way to ease your own.

Dickens pushed aside the déjà vu, but it was like pushing aside water. A new feeling rushed in like a flash flood. It had lurked below the surface, but now floated to the top:

Discomfort, at the sight of the Revision Room. Discomfort beyond just awkward, unpleasant. This discomfort felt like a form of torture, perpetrated by the room's aesthetics. It was drab. Beyond drab. But well lit. Too well lit. Bright lights installed with purpose, as if an interior designer were hired to cultivate this air of discomfort. Dickens fought discomfort with his slight sense of:

Amusement, at what the building might have looked like from the outside. It must have been an enormous concrete brick, boring every person who walked past. Of course, since the building didn't have a single window, that he ever saw, it could have been at the bottom of the ocean.

He hadn't even seen the outside world, other than peeks from videos during The Orientation. Wait? Maybe he had seen the outside world? He couldn't remember. His memory was worse than he ever remembered in his Birth Life, and details of his Resurrection Life, before The Orientation, were just random, disjointed snap shots.

Dickens recalled waking up on a bed, encircled with people wearing white lab coats, overwhelmingly white lab coats. In the next snap shot, he was wheeled into a corridor and down to a room resembling a jail cell, except for its blinding white walls. The third snap shot was of being warned he might experience a "slight" headache. An understatement, since his skull felt like it was split open and held together with a vice.

Was that what happened? Perhaps at some point his skull had been held together with a vice. He had been brought back from the dead. Who knows what that entailed? Maybe that was part of the process? No! He would have remembered that, right?

He doubted himself. Did any of that really happen? He wasn't certain, and his uncertainty threatened to grow into debilitating confusion if he didn't stop it. He forced himself to redirect his mind to something that amused him during The Orientation: sitting in front of an enormous movie screen, watching a video called "So, You've Been Resurrected."

The video featured a striking spokeswoman, who Dickens, at first, thought talked directly to him, but discovered it was prerecorded when he attempted to ask a question. With a glimmering smile, she explained that he was brought back to life thanks to a state-of-the-art Machine. Currently the group who owned this one-of-a-kind, top-secret Machine, was utilizing it to Resurrect the most influential writers throughout history, honoring them with an opportunity to Revise their works.

Dickens allowed his amusement to step aside as:

Curiosity, moved front and center. Curiosity about why they were doing this. How they rationalized it. Was there anything he could gain by replaying this explanation in his mind?

While maintaining an absurdly wide smile, the spokeswoman explained that it was reasonable for him to think it "wrong" or perhaps even "sinful" to secretly alter classic literature and philosophical texts. The Revision Oversight Team understood this, since the concepts of truth during his Birth Life weren't as advanced.

He died before the discovery of Ultimate Truth, but, being one of the most brilliant thinkers of all time, he would learn quickly. He would realize it as something that was hiding in plain sight his entire Birth Life, but soon, he would be eager to "enhance the original language" of his book and "amend his original intent."

She further explained that Modern Truth Proponents believe that, on occasion, tampering with reality is necessary for Ultimate Truth to prevail. Facts, including historical facts, are often barriers to Ultimate Truth. This, she said, might be difficult for him to grasp, but the following examples should make the basic concept clear:

Example 1: He was told to imagine a friend buys a pair of shoes. The friend, who is emotionally sensitive, can't stop talking about how much he loves his new shoes. Then, unfortunately, the friend asks whether you like them. In this example, you hate his shoes. So, if you answered, "Yes, I like them," that would, technically, be a lie. However, if you tell the truth, he'd be crushed. Therefore, a truth adjustment is justified. By telling him you like the shoes, you are actually saying, "your friendship is more valuable than my opinion." That statement is true, which means your "lie" was literally used to communicate an even higher form of truth. This is an example of Ultimate Truth.

Example 2: He was told to imagine a biologist wrote a book filled with falsehoods about the origins of life. This book misleads millions of scientists, who end up conducting studies based on these falsehoods, resulting in further falsehoods about the origins of human life. This leads some to doubt the existence of an omnipotent creator. Eventually, our children could begin to doubt the existence of an omnipotent creator. This biologist's book has caused irreparable harm to our children's relationship with the creator of the universe, just like your truth about the shoes would have caused irreparable harm to your relationship with your friend. Therefore, Resurrecting the biologist and forcing him to Revise his book is, obviously, a justified truth adjustment. The Revision would communicate the higher form of truth, which is another example of Ultimate Truth.

The woman in the video stated, proponents of the Modern Truth Movement are justified in making truth adjustments if they are a barrier between mankind and the Ultimate Truth. Not doing so would be a betrayal to Ultimate Truth, which in turn, would mean you are bearing false witness to your neighbor. In other words, if one chooses NOT to alter these "Barrier Facts," that person has broken the 9th Commandment. Those who DO alter the Barrier Facts, not only obey the commandment, but play a role in creating Ultimate Truth.

The Revision Oversight Team, being honorable and honest people, had chosen not to Revise the works themselves. Once they had caught word of the invention of the Resurrection Machine, they pursued ownership of the Machine, and acquired it by a means that would remain classified. She assured him it was obtained "honorably" as God had "shown them great favor." The Machine presented them the opportunity to facilitate the Revision without compromising their principles.

Dickens knew he needed to navigate his mind in another direction. Ruminating on this philosophy would cause swelling, from anger and frustration, plaguing his mind like an itch he'd never scratch. He alleviated this swelling by reflecting on the movies he had watched, bringing on a sense of:

Appreciation, for the films he was forced to view, but genuinely enjoyed watching. Pretty Woman, The Sixth Sense, Lethal Weapon, Wall Street, Red Dawn, The Hangover (which he loved), Ferris Bueller's Day Off, and Die Hard, were the ones he remembered watching.

Dickens' mood improved, thinking about the movies. Modern America couldn't be entirely bad. The movies reflected values that didn't align with the Modern Truth Movement. He wondered if any of his books were turned into films, and how fun it would be to watch one. It gave him a tiny bit of:

Hope, which brought a truce for the emotional civil war in his mind. He wasn't sure how long he'd stopped typing while lost in thought. He felt like he'd already lucked out by not getting in trouble, so he started up his two-finger tapping again, shifting his attention back to what was happening as Ebenezer Scrooge entered his house.

***

The door slammed behind me, echoing throughout the house. My senses were heightened and as I made my way down the hall and climbed the staircase, I could hear every time my shoe tapped the floor and every creak from the aging wood beneath me. I told myself: Nothing to be startled about. Just sound waves being amplified by the emptiness of the house.

I also had never made note of how dark the place was. On that night, the space was visually opaque until I lit my candle, which only illuminated what was within arm's length.

The darkness was intentional. Darkness was cheap. And on most nights the darkness wouldn't have even crossed my mind. But, obviously, this night was different.

I walked with my candle in hand through every room in the house. Searching for what? I don't know. I wanted to see if anything else was out of the ordinary. I saw nothing out of order. Nobody hiding under a table or behind a curtain. All rooms were as I'd left them that morning, so after that, I walked upstairs to my bedroom, closed the heavy door, and applied every lock.

***

A window popped up on Dickens' monitor, screaming, "Boredom alert," in bright yellow letters.

Boredom? He took a few deep breaths, attempting to calm down, as he continued reading the fine print below the warning, which said: "You are going into way too much detail and failing to get to the point. Please refrain from all the fruity details."

Defiance boiled up within him. Pounding his keyboard, as if it was responsible for the insult, he made Scrooge say:

***

"I was a jerk. I met some ghosts. I learned some stuff. I bought a goose. Two cheers for Christmas! THE END*"*

***

As Dickens looked at his words, satisfaction washed over him. It was fabulous. Sarcastic disobedience at its best. He was damn proud of it — for a few seconds. Pride yielded to feelings of futility.

Defiance felt good, but it obviously wouldn't help. He would have to be clever. Could there be a way for him to signal to his more astute readers that this was a phony, fake Revision? Could he clue readers in, maybe blow the lid off this entire Revision project, in a way that his captors wouldn't detect? Suddenly, he was filled with ideas on how to make that happen. He returned to abusing his keyboard.

***

~~"I was a jerk. I met some ghosts. I learned some stuff. I bought a goose. Two cheers for Christmas! THE END"~~

Once the door was locked, I removed my clothing and put on my nightgown — Yes, I wear a nightgown! Even worse, I wear a nightcap — But that doesn't mean I, Ebenezer Scrooge, wasn't dripping with sex appeal.

Sure, I looked like an idiot. But over the course of the next 180 years, or so, I bet people wear dumber shit than that. I predict denim shorts will eventually be in style, as ridiculous as that sounds.

I took a seat near the fireplace and began eating my gruel.

Wait! Hang on.

(Hey! You. The reader. Yes, you! The person reading these words right now: Didn't I mention earlier that I had dinner at the tavern? I think I just discovered a continuity error in my own writing. Fuck! That's embarrassing!)

Wait! I had a cold or something. It wasn't my dinner. I was eating gruel because I was sick.

(Hey! Reader! Did I mention that I was sick that night? Are did I delete that part? Regardless, I was sick with a cold that night., which makes me wonder if I, you know, Ebenezer Scrooge, not the author Charles Dickens, mind you, was having a crazy fever dream when I saw all the ghosts. A cold could cause that, right? If the whole thing was just a dream, I'm not sure this story's worth telling.)

Anyway, moving on … I was sitting by the fire and it was cold, so I sat close.

(Hey! Reader! It appears that, in my original version, I described the shit out of the fireplace. Doesn't add much to the scene, does it? So, I'm going to cut it out in this rewrite I'm being forced to …)

***

Dickens stopped typing. He was getting carried away. His captors were dimwits, but these dimwits had access to some highly-sophisticated software capable of detecting boring writing. He would have to be both clever, and subtle.

***

Doesn't add much to the scene, does it? So, I'm going to cut it out in this rewrite I'm being forced to …)

I heard the cellar door creak open, followed by chains dragging across the floor. The noise grew louder and louder, and then, accompanied by footsteps, moved up the stairs, and up to the door.

"It's bullshit!" I said. "I won't believe it."

(Hey! My very smart, and discerning reader: would you not agree this was a dumb thing for me to say? I mean, "believe" what? Clearly some weird shit was going on, but I'd already drawn the conclusion that I was about to see a ghost when all I'd heard were footsteps. I should have been more concerned about an intruder. Right? Isn't that a more logical assumption?)

***

Dickens stopped typing, suppressing a laugh. This was getting silly, directly addressing the reader like that. Not only was it silly, it was confusing.

Would readers think it was Scrooge addressing them? Or would they think it was Dickens? His intent was for it to be Scrooge, as the writer, talking to the reader. But if that were the case, why is he being forced to rewrite the story, which was originally in third person?

It didn't matter. He'd eventually have to rewrite the section. There's no way something this brazen would slip past his captors.

Unless … no one actually ends up reading this. They designed this software to keep Revisions on track, but, what if no one else reads it? A distinct possibility, since none of these people seemed the literary type. And, so far, the software wasn't flagging any of this.

He decided it was worth the risk. Using the word "fuck" had been his lone source of enjoyment, but now, he was enjoying addressing the reader. His remaining "fucks" would run out soon, so, what the hell?

"Fuck it!" Dickens whispered, as he resumed typing.

***

However, my dear reader, this ill-conceived foreshadowing proved correct, as right before my eyes, I saw the ghost of my stone-fucking dead business partner, Jacob Marley. He carried heaps of chains, so many that, if they were pulled tight, he would have looked like a chain-linked mummy.

Attached to his chains were various office supplies: a cash box, keys, padlocks, ledgers, deeds, etc. (I'd always wondered where that stuff went). I could see right through him, much like every ghost you've ever seen in a movie, which didn't exist at the time of this writing.

Even though it was obvious the ghost of Marley had strolled into my bedroom, I was inexplicably still unconvinced.

"What do you want from me?" I asked, in a dickish tone.

"All kinds of stuff," Marley's ghost said, in the voice Marley had when he was alive, which is really not worth pointing out. Is it? But it's too late now.

Despite knowing the answer, I asked, "Who are you?"

"Ask me who I was," Marley said, which was a pretty cool line, no? I'm still proud of that one.

"Who were you then?" I said, loudly.

"I was your partner, Jacob Marley."

"Would you please have a seat?" I asked.

(Huh? Why would I need him to sit down? What's the point? Clearly, I was phoning it in during this scene. BTW: phones didn't exist either, at the time of this writing.)

"I can," Marley said.

"Do it, then," I said.

(Oh! I explained it a little later. Oops! Should have just kept reading. My bad. I asked him to sit down because: a ghost might not be able to sit in a chair. He'd slipped right through the door, so I wanted to see if he could sit down without falling to the floor. Eh! Explanation's kind of weak. Sorry about that. I'll try to not suck so bad at writing from this point forward.)

***

Dickens stopped typing as he saw The Supervisor getting chewed out by his boss, The Overseer. They pointed in his direction as they spoke, but he couldn't hear them. Dickens could see a vein pulsing from The Overseer's forehead from across the room, and he could only assume his obvious attempts to address the reader had prompted this anger.

The Overseer walked away in a huff, and, a moment after, Dickens saw The Supervisor storming toward his cubicle. He braced himself for a verbal pounding.

"Mr. Dickens," The Supervisor said, in a condescending, boss-like tone.

"Yes sir?" Dickens said, higher pitched than expected.

"Your writing has triggered a number of warnings," he said, "and we need to address them."

"Of course," Dickens said, feigning ignorance. "What needs to be addressed?"

"I don't care about the cussin'," he said, trying to sound like a cool boss. "We can fix that with a search and replace. No biggie!"

"Yes, sir," Dickens said. "I understand."

"I'll get you a list of modern cuss words," he said, "and a list of words to replace them with."

"Very well."

"All I ask is you don't get me in trouble," The Supervisor said, sternly. "You follow?"

"Oh, yes, sir," Dickens said, sarcastically, which The Supervisor didn't detect. "The last thing I want to do is get you in trouble."

"Good," he said. "I'm glad we have an understanding."

The Supervisor crossed his arms, staring intensely.

"Mr. Dickens," he said, "you need to take the boredom warnings seriously. Boredom is not easy to fix."

The Supervisor's face grew red with anger, as he said, "you can't search and replace boring writing!"

Dickens nodded in agreement.

"The Editor says boredom will not be tolerated," he said. "Whenever that warning pops up, please go back and delete all boring words."

"How am I supposed to determine which words are boring?" he asked.

"Look, I'm just a Revision Room supervisor," he said, smirking. "You are one of the most famous writers of all time. Which one of us should be better at spotting boring words?"

Dickens returned with a smile, he fancied himself a humble man, but being referred to as "one of the most famous writers of all time" did stroke his ego.

"Of course, sir," Dickens said.

"Good," The Supervisor said. "Boredom gets me in trouble. And what is the worst thing you can do in my division?"

"Get YOU in trouble," he said, dripping with sarcasm.

"That's right," he said. "But you did a superb job on that whole part about taxes. The Revision Oversight Team loved that."

"Thank you, sir," Dickens said.

The Supervisor gave him another way-too-hard pat on the back. Was he doing it too hard on purpose? Or did he not know it was unpleasant for the recipient?

The Supervisor walked off, and Dickens looked back at his screen.

"They don't like too many words," Nietzsche said, whispering. "When I Revised 'Beyond Good and Evil', that Boredom Warning popped up after every sentence."

"Is that right?" Dickens asked.

"Yes," Nietzsche said. "The final draft was 10 pages. Who knows what happened once The Editor saw it."

He was about to ask for more information about The Editor, but he caught an unhappy glance from The Supervisor and held back.

Dickens still didn't understand the editorial workflow. It sounded like somebody was reading along as he wrote. Someone located elsewhere. If they were, they seemed to be only catching bits and pieces. Was there a way to tell when someone was reading along?

As this thought sunk in, he accepted that addressing the reader was a bad idea. So far it was slipping passed the software, but it wouldn't slip past even the most incompetent editor. Too bad. He enjoyed addressing the reader, but, on the bright side, his boss flat out told him he didn't care about language.

To alert the reader, though, he would have to be cunning. Maybe if he attempted to slip in his personal values, as long as they didn't interfere with the purpose of the Revision, and also, apparently, not bore people, it might work. With this new plan in mind, he continued writing.

***

"I'm sitting right in front of you," the Ghost said. "You see me. Hear me. You might even catch a whiff of rotting flesh. Why are you not trusting your senses?"

"Because," I said, "My senses can fail me. You may be a hunk of undigested beef, a glob of mustard, a morsel of an undercooked potato. You have more in common with gravy than you do the grave!"

"What the fuck are you talking about?" the Ghost said.

He made a good point. This was not sound reasoning.

The Ghost stood up, bellowed out a scary ghost sound, and rattled his chains. It freaked me the fuck out.

"Please have mercy," I yelled, falling to my knees.

"Okay," the Ghost said. "You believe I'm real now?"

"Yes," I said. "You are real. But, for fuck sake, why are you bothering me?"

"Oh! Sorry. I guess I skipped that part," he said, switching to a more formal, ghost-like tone. "I am here because it is required of every man to travel far and wide, committing works of charity and kindness for his fellowman. If that spirit does not go forth in life, he is condemned to do so after death. I was doomed to wander across Earth upon my death — oh, woe is me!"

I just looked at him, confused.

"In short," The Ghost said, "I was a prick in life. Men aren't supposed to be pricks, you see. We are supposed to help one another. And if you don't do that while you're alive, you'll do it when you're dead."

**

Dickens stopped writing. He'd wanted to show that people shouldn't be greedy, and should be kind to one another, but wondered if making it a requirement was the best way to go. If people start doing kind acts only to avoid punishment in the afterlife, they might do acts that appear nice but don't actually help.

Giving money just for a tax break. Donating things to charity that no one needs. Ladling food to the hungry just to be seen. What he really wanted was for people to change, really change, their hearts and minds. To care for one another, not out of fear, but out of genuine love for their fellow man.

But Dickens feared he'd regret making too many changes to this scene. It could potentially ruin upcoming plot points. Best to not risk it. He decided to press on.

Besides, he DID know what happened when a person died, and that was information he probably shouldn't share.

***

"The chains I wear around me," the Ghost bellowed. "I made it link by link. I created it with the decisions I made while I was alive."

I shook in terror.

"And you think these chains are burdensome," the Ghost said. "Just wait until you see the chains that await YOU."

"If that's the case," I asked. "Why did you wait seven years?"

"You know?" The Ghost said, getting pissed. "I didn't have to come at all. No one came to ME with a warning."

"Weren't you required to do this?" I asked.

"No," the Ghost said. "I have suffered these last 7 years, and it has instilled in me an appreciation for the suffering of others. Ebenezer, you suffer none now, but my visit to you tonight is to warn you of the suffering you WILL experience."

"I HAVE suffered," I said.

"Riiiiiight," the Ghost said, sarcastic. "You have to pay taxes with money you have no intention of spending. That's not suffering, you dipshit."

"But you were good," I said. "A great man of business."

"Business?" the Ghost cried. "Helping out my fellow man was my business. Charity was my business. Kindness, mercy, and empathy was my business. The 'business' I conducted for a living …"

He flashed uber-sarcastic air quotes when he said "business."

"… was not my actual 'business'."

I failed to understand this train of thought, but I was too scared to argue.

"The only way the 'business' I conducted would have applied to my real 'business,'" Marley said, still flashing air quotes, "would have been for me to take all of that money and give it to the poor."

I began to shake violently, not out of the horror of beholding the ghost of my stone-fucking dead business partner, but of the thought of taking my hard-earned money and handing it over to freeloading, piece-of-shit poor people.

"Ebenezer," the Ghost said, "direct your attention to the suffering of others. You must understand the suffering of others. AND do whatever is within your means to help ease that suffering."

"Is there a way I can do that and still keep my money?" I pleaded.

The Ghost looked disappointed, which is saying a lot for a ghost.

"Ebenezer," he said. "I can see we're getting nowhere. Let's try another approach."

"Yes?" I asked, hoping that giving away money would not be part of this next approach.

"You will be haunted," the Ghost said, "by Three Spirits."

"Oh," I said, disappointed. "That's your new approach? More hauntings?"

"Yes!" he said.

"Um, you know what?" I said. "I'll roll the dice on this whole suffering thing."

"Oh, God," he said. "Ebenezer, your ignorance about suffering is worse than I thought."

I didn't respond to this, hoping he'd give up.

Marley continued, "Nevertheless, I do understand suffering, and, out of empathy for your future self, I will have these ghosts haunt you."

I rolled my eyes, and said, "Fine! But can I meet with them all at once? Get this shit over with?"

"Expect the first ghost when the clock strikes 1 a.m.," he said, ignoring my question. "The other two will show up … you know what? The ghosts will show up whenever the fuck they want."

He gathered his chains under one arm and walked over to the window. With his free hand, Marley extended his middle finger as he floated out into the night.

I had grown so weary, stressing about the possibility of losing my money, I felt I could slip into a coma. I staggered over to my bed, made an ungraceful belly-flop, and fell fast asleep.

***

Dickens was pleased with himself. He'd managed to get across some of his personal values and avoided additional warnings from the software. His artistic integrity and love for his readers was still strong, even under the circumstances. Also, unlike addressing the reader directly, this tactic could actually work.

A steam whistle blew. It sent chills up his spine, stoking painful childhood memories of toiling away in a blacking factory.

"Okay, Revisers," The Supervisor said, standing up and stretching his back. "It's break time."

The other Revisers removed their hairpieces, stood up, and filtered into a break room on one side of the Revision Room, or into a restroom on the opposite side. Eerily, no one made a sound. He was dying to figure out the identity of the other clean-shaved, bald-headed Revisers, but he assumed there was a reason no one talked.

Still on edge from the last time he stood up, he felt it best to stay seated. The Supervisor began motioning for him to stand up, after which he removed his hairpiece and facial hair, and headed toward the break room after the others.

A few moments later, Dickens sat in the break room, in awe of the vending machines. Fellow workers — some wearing CRC jumpsuits, and others wearing modern clothing — fed money into the vending machines, made their selections, waited for their selection to drop, and walked away as if nothing monumental had happened. Most of the technology he'd encountered in his Resurrection Life overwhelmed him, but the vending machines didn't. He understood them and their purpose immediately, which is why he found them so fascinating.

Dickens had picked a bag of cheese-dusted corn chips and a sugary carbonated beverage served in a metal can. Both seemed good, at first. After eating his third chip, he hated the way the cheese dust stuck to his fingers. After his fourth sip of the soda, he'd reached his limit with its syrupy sweetness. He couldn't understand how the modern-dressed people gulped their snacks and slurped their sodas, as if unaware they were consuming anything.

He was eager to learn more about vending machines and how prevalent they were in modern society. Maybe modern man purchased his clothing in similar machines, adding money and selecting their respective sizes. Were books ordered in this fashion, too? What about medicine? Picture frames? Teacups? Perhaps people could purchase their own vending machine out of giant vending machine.

Did vending machines exist in homes? Did women still cook dinner for their families, or did they have vending machines in their kitchens? He grew excited at the idea of vending machines providing his favorite items, such as cigars and brandy.

A troubling thought occurred to him. "People" accomplished these tasks, in his day. People made food. People sold brandy and cigars. Tasks people needed so their families were fed. Perhaps this technological advancement, much like those during his Birth Life, created incredible wealth for a few people, but sent far more people into poverty. A means of making a living is too often erased in the name of convenience.

In his day, technological advancements drove men going into lives of thievery, and women into lives of prostitution. He wondered: "What if a vending machine could fulfill the need men had for prostitutes?"

This created a visualization that made him want to poke out his mind's eye. His brain was creating thoughts so abhorrent, he forced himself to push them away, dwelling on the first thing that popped in his head: The objective of his Revision.

At the demand of his captors, Dickens' objective for this Revision of "A Christmas Carol "was to: 1) Punch up the writing and make it appeal more to the modern reader; 2) Avoid any blatant bashing of business; 3) Tell the story from Ebenezer Scrooge's point of view to help illustrate how difficult it can be for a wealthy, "job-creating" man, whom the mooching class feels justified in persecuting. 4) Change Scrooge's lesson in the end into something Christmas-themed.

For branding purposes, they would likely keep the book's original title, but he was told to Revise the book as if it were titled, "A Capitalist Carol." But regardless what their marketing people chose to do with the title, the new subtitle would be: "The heroic tale of Ebenezer Scrooge and that free-loading Bob Cratchit."

He'd laughed when he heard the subtitle, assuming it was a joke. It wasn't. None of this was a joke.

Thinking about the objective of the Revision, led him right back to horrible thoughts about poverty. He imagined the sorrow of the poor children in this modern society. Children whose families may not be able to afford their own vending machines, and therefore must suffer through lives of thievery, prostitution, or worse.

The steam whistle blew again, marking the end of his break. Unlike before, this sound was a relief from the upsetting thoughts swirling within his mind. He debated for a moment about whether to scarf down his remaining chips and soda. The thought made him sick, so he tossed them in a trash bin. His brain was already generating more nausea than he could handle.

Dickens returned to his cubicle and readied himself to start the next chapter in the world of the "heroic" Mr. Scrooge.

CHAPTER 2: THE FIRST OF THE THREE SPIRITS

or
I MEAN, 'FIRST SPIRIT' IF YOU DON'T COUNT
MY STONE-FUCKING DEAD BUSINESS PARTNER

I woke up suddenly, as a light flashed, and standing before me was a strange figure. It was short, had pure white hair, and the features of an old person, but with skin as smooth as a child. It had holly wrapped around it, which made it look all Christmas-ish.

We all know what it was, don't we? The first ghost. I, apparently, still felt the need to ask.

"Are you the spirit Marley told me would come?" *I asked.*

"Uh, no shit, you dooooooooouche!" *it said, in a tone that sounded like a person doing a bad impression of a ghost.* "You're a fucking genius."

"Who ... I mean, what are you?" *I asked, in no mood for mockery.*

"I am the Ghost of Christmas Past."

"Past? Like the history of Christmas?" *I asked, confused.*

"Nooooooo," the ghost said, sounding, again, like the "ooooooooh" of a kid on Halloween wearing a bed sheet with holes cut out for eyes. "Your past."

I had to shield my eyes from the glow of the Ghost's white outfit, which illuminated as if it were being hit with a spotlight.

It held a lampshade in its hands.

"Dude," I said to the Ghost. "You're blinding the fuck out of me. Could you cover yourself with that lampshade?"

"Noooooooooooo," the Ghost said. "I'm going to reveal things you have not been able to see. I'm going to shine a light on that which you have willfully been in the dark about."

The Ghost dropped the ghost-like voice, and bluntly said, "Get it? I'm shining a light both physically and metaphorically?"

"Yes," I said, losing my patience. "But why are you doing this to me?"

"It will do you goooooooood," the Ghost said, returning to the Halloween-ghost-sounding tone.

"You know what would do me some good?" I asked. "Some fucking sleep."

The Ghost ignored this, and said, "This is for your welfare, for you are very poor …"

"Welfare?" I said, abruptly. "I'm rich. I can't go on welfare."

"Pooooooor in spirit," the Ghost said. "Soooooo, shut the fuck up, and come with me."

The Ghost reached out and took my hand. Its hand was tiny but had the strength of a bodybuilder.

I was trying to think of a good excuse to get out of this. Crappy weather? I'm wearing my pajamas? I have a "thing" in the morning? Obviously, no excuse would work. So, I pretty much had to go along.

We walked together to the window, and it seemed as if the Ghost wanted us to jump out.

"Please!" I pleaded. "If I jump out the window with you I will fall to my death."

"Come ooooooooon," the ghost howled. "Stop being such a puuuuuuussy."

As the spirit glided forward, the wall drew back before us, like a curtain opening at the beginning of a play. On the other side, it was daytime, clear, and snow was on the ground. We were standing on a country road with large pastureland on either side.

"Holy shit!" I said. "This is where I grew up."

The Ghost rolled its eyes at me for stating the obvious. I ignored this, as the smells filled my senses, prompting a rush of feelings to return. Feelings of hope. Joy. Optimism. Feelings I hadn't experienced in ages.

"You're shaking," the Ghost said. "And what's that on your cheek?"

I moved my hand up to my face and realized I had developed a pimple.

***

"Huh?" Dickens whispered, to himself, pulling away from the screen for a moment. "I gave Scrooge a pimple? What was the point of that?"

It wasn't really funny, so it couldn't be that. Old Scrooge wasn't putting on young Scrooge's clothes. Furthermore, it's weird, with far more unusual things occurring that evening, for him to experience embarrassment.

"Embarrassment! Of Course!" Dickens said to himself, but loud enough for those around him to hear. A few people turned their heads, but then went back to their work.

Dickens remembered that he wanted Scrooge to remember what it was like to feel embarrassment, as he did when he was that age.

"I like that," he muttered. "But the purpose isn't clear."

He decided to make it clear.

***

"You're shaking," the Ghost said, smirking. Pointing toward my face, he asked, "What's that on your cheek?"

I felt my face and realized I had developed a pimple. An emotion rushed over me I hadn't felt in years: Embarrassment. I pretended to lightly scratch my face just above the pimple, in an awkward attempt to cover it. Feeling embarrassed for a pimple, especially in front of a ghost, only made my embarrassment grow stronger within me. But it is exactly what I experienced at that age, when I lived along this country road. Despite the flash flood of feelings I encountered during that phase of my life, embarrassment always floated to the top.

The Ghost lost the smirk, and asked, "Do you remember the rest of the way?"

"Yes!" I shouted, louder than intended. "I could get us there with my eyes closed."

"It's interesting you can remember so well," the Ghost said, mocking, "not having been here in sooooooooo many years."

I felt a blast of warmth on my face, as it turned bright red from embarrassment. It's odd to experience child-like humiliation after being called old, and it was an exceptionally hurtful jab since, you know, it came from a ghost. But my excitement to see my old stomping grounds was strong, too.

I remembered every detail along our walk: every tree, fencepost, and even a few bales of hay seemed familiar. An icy creek ran across the road, above which a picturesque bridge was built.

A caravan of horses rushed by, ridden by my former classmates. I fought the urge to cover up my pimple from them as they flew past, appearing to be happy and cheerful. They didn't see us, which made me feel insignificant, leading to a pang of hurt and embarrassment.

I waved "hello" to get their attention.

"They aren't real, you knoooooow?" the Ghost said.

"Are they ghosts, too?" I asked.

"Noooooooo," the Ghost said, "they're more like shadows trapped in time."

"What do you mean?" I asked. "How are they trapped?"

"That might not be the best way to explain it," the Ghost said, contemplating. "But one thing's for certain, they can't see you or hear you. I'm a ghost, not a fucking time machine."

Regardless, I was happy to see them all again, and was even happy to hear them all singing repulsive Christmas songs.

We continued our walk toward the small schoolhouse and moved into the building through a wall, which seemed unnecessary, since the door was right there, but I dismissed that thought when I saw a young boy sitting alone at his desk.

"Hmmmmm," the Ghost howled. "There is a boy sitting here all by himself."

It was me, which I knew as soon as we stepped in, but when we walked around to the front of the room, and I saw the look on my previous self's face, a wave of childhood hurt feelings began to build in my chest, and tears welled up in my eyes

"Is this boy choosing to be alone?" the Ghost asked. "Or do the other boys not like him?"

I shrugged, even though I knew the answer.

"Maybe the other boys think he's a loser," the Ghost said. "Or perhaps they find his personality off-putting. Or maybe it's his haircut …"

"Enough!" I shouted, growing furious. "They didn't like me, but I never understood why."

I realized the boys I'd been so happy to see minutes before were the very ones who'd rejected me. They'd really hurt me, and that hurt remained as fresh as it was back then. I suppose this meant I'd been living with these wounds ever since, though the memory lay far beneath memories deposited from other eras.

I found myself wanting to cover up my pimple again, but before I could, the ghost grabbed my hand. The wall opened, again, like a curtain, revealing we were stepping into a mansion.

We walked our way through the mansion, and another wave of long-forgotten feelings swept over me. The mansion was enormous, but had been neglected, badly, for quite some time. Windows were broken. Moss grew on walls. Dust piled so thick atop mantels the color of wood was no longer identifiable. It was as if a decorator had been hired to make it feel even drearier.

In a large parlor, a boy sat, me, a year or two older, beside a fireplace reading a book. Feelings I had not felt in eons swelled up in me like a balloon. Creativity. Wonder. Inspiration. The feelings of being immersed in a good book, letting my imagination take over.

A parade of fictional characters, or the way I envisioned them, marched through the parlor. Ali Baba. Robinson Crusoe. Don Quixote. Side characters from these books filed in, leading in others I'd invented myself, figments of my childhood imagination.

The enjoyment of this scene wore off as the characters began to fade, and eventually disappeared altogether. The sadness of a lonesome childhood rose within my chest, making it difficult to breathe. The mansion was in shambles due to neglect, and, I, my boyhood self, was clearly in shambles for the same reason.

The fictional characters had often been my only friends. My only family. Imaginary friends are sad companions on Christmas day. This compelled me to sit down beside my childhood self and weep, wishing there were a way to bring him comfort.

***

Dickens stopped typing. He had no recollection of writing or even reading the scene with young Scrooge immersed in an imaginary world on Christmas day. Oddly, it was as if he were reading this scene for the first time. Was it something that had never really stood out to him? Or maybe a scene his readers never asked him about? Or perhaps it was his post-Resurrection brain fog at work, once again?

Regardless, he enjoyed the scene. He liked the idea of showing why Scrooge had turned into, well, Scrooge, showing that villains among us were often also, at least at some point in their lives, victims. They were human, and it was important to continue to portray them as human.

Dickens inferred that, when writing this scene, he must have had empathy for young Ebenezer Scrooge. Who could read this scene and not empathize with this innocent, lonely child? But that can't justify him growing up into such a horrible person, right? The mansion wasn't pleasant to look at, but Scrooge's situation was better than children living on the streets. And let's not forget young Scrooge was READING on Christmas day, giving him a means of coping with loneliness many children didn't have. A neglected child, rich or poor, is deserving of our sympathies, but a child with food, shelter, and an education likely wouldn't suffer his entire life.

Dickens had met many "Scrooges" in his Birth Life, who SHOULD have empathized with those who suffer but, instead, viewed the poor as lazy, selfish, losers. Many had attitudes of "I made something of myself, why can't you?" For them, paying higher taxes, or as in Scrooge's case, throwing a little money toward a charity, wasn't fair. Ending the needless suffering of others wasn't a value unto itself. They believed suffering was the fault of those who suffer, since they should have, simply, made themselves rich.

"Why didn't I turn out like that?" Dickens thought to himself. "What made me recognize these injustices, even when I no longer suffered?"

Dickens' upbringing wasn't exactly like the other children raised in poverty. His father did, at one time, have an important job, made decent money, and socialized in upper-class circles. His father's recklessness with money caused the hard times of his childhood, as he attempted to live beyond his means. Despite his decent income, he'd borrowed from every friend and family member able to lend him money. He rarely paid any of it back, though. This led to epic rifts in his extended family, and his carelessness, ultimately, drove Dickens' father into debtor's prison.

Even though there was tremendous suffering in Dickens' childhood, it wasn't as if he didn't have advantages. Extended family members also were educated and financially well off, and the behavior of successful and educated relatives must rub off on children. How could it not? This certainly provides knowledge just as beneficial to one's success as formal education, and well-connected relatives present significant advantages in the "who you know" department.

Dickens understood poverty from poor people's standpoint, understood poverty from an upper-class standpoint, and understood the truth about why some suffered and why some didn't. This helped in his decision to pursue a career as a writer instead of a career in parliament, as some expected him to do as a young man, knowing the key to progress lay in changes needed in people's minds. Depicting the humanity of those who suffer in poverty was the most potent way Dickens knew how to do this.

He'd trailed off into this thought a tad too deeply, and needed to push it aside, for now, and move ahead with the Revision and his plan to undermine it. Degrees of suffering was a good thing for readers to ponder, and since Dickens' captors weren't allowing him to portray Scrooge, in the end, as learning a lesson about the suffering greed can cause, he could at least allow the selfish asshole to do some meaningful reflecting.

***

"This," I said, pointing toward my former self, "is a sad childhood. But not as sad as the childhoods I willingly ignore every day."

The Ghost slowly nodded in agreement.

"I suppose," I said, "blind spots, like these, are what you intended to illuminate with your brightness."

The Ghost smiled. Pointing in another direction, he said, "Let us see another Christmas."

***

Dickens smiled. He felt as if he was making improvements to his book, which was an impressive feat since the book was already a classic.

"I've still got it!" he said to himself.

***

Again, the walls drew back like curtains, and we were in the main hall of the boarding school on, I think, Christmas the following year. I saw my boyhood self, standing in the middle of the room pacing back and forth.

My current, old-man self, looked around the room, remembering tiny details about the main hall — lovely crown molding, eerie paintings, musty smells — I'd long forgotten. At first it had a pleasant nostalgic feeling, but, suddenly, I started to grow nervous. I couldn't quite remember what was about to happen, but, somehow, I knew something big was about to transpire, as I mindlessly directed my attention to the entrance.

The door flew open and a little girl, much younger than my boyhood self, ran into the room, threw her arms around me, and said, "Ebenezer, my dear brother."

I felt faint at this sight. I grabbed the edge of a nearby table to steady myself.

"Fanny?" my boyhood self said, genuinely surprised. "What are you doing here?"

"I am here to take you home!" the girl said with a beaming smile. "Home! Home! Home!"

"Home?" I repeated.

"Yes," Fanny said, delighted. "Home forever and ever. Father isn't mean anymore. I asked him last night if you could come home, and he said 'Yes.'"

My boyhood self was too shocked to respond.

Fanny laughed and jumped up and down. She then, in an adorable, child-like way, grasped my hand and attempted to drag me toward the door. I saw a very amused and joyous smile form across my face, as I'd allowed her to drag me along.

"She really was something," the Ghost said. "Delicate. But with a large heart."

"Oh, yes," I said.

"She died as a young woman," the Ghost said. "But not before she bore children."

"One child," I said.

"Yes, of course," the Ghost said. "Your nephew."

I swallowed loudly and said, "Yes."

"Do you still see him?" the Ghost asked.

"I saw him this afternoon," I said, with great embarrassment of how I'd treated my dear Fanny's one and only child.

***

Dickens stopped typing, lowered his head, and said to himself, "Oh my God. Fanny!" In all of the perplexity of his Resurrection and the Revision, it hadn't occurred to him until now that everyone he knew had also been dead for over a hundred years — including his sister Fanny. He had considered it a nice gesture to name Scrooge's beloved sister (and other characters in other novels) after his own sister, and it gave him a hint of pride that his sister's name was alive and well in this character. But it also made him miss her.

There was no way any of his loved ones were still alive. His wife and children included.

No friends. No acquaintances. No enemies.

It was a terribly depressing thought, but what could he do? Nothing. Mourn the loss of people to whom he'd already said goodbye?

It was unlikely his captors would allow him to take off the rest of the day to mourn his deceased loved ones, so he tried to find a way to push the reality of this out of his mind or at least redirect it toward something else. But then it occurred to him, "Wait! I must have grandchildren," he said under his breath. "Hundreds of them."

His motivation took on a more realistic feeling as he thought about his great, great, great, great grandchildren, and how his descendants were alive in this horrible world. He fantasized about imaginary grandchildren, ones he could bounce on his knee and tell stories about what things were like in his day.

It was a stretch to imagine grandchildren he could know in this way, but he ignored that thought. He needed to find ways to survive this place. With these imaginary grandchildren in mind, he began typing with refreshed fervor.

**

The schoolhouse began to fill with fog so thick we could no longer see our surroundings, but after it dissipated, we were no longer in the school, but were standing in the busy thoroughfare of a city.

The Ghost asked, "Do you recognize this place?"

"Recognize it?" I said. "I was an apprentice here."

We walked in and saw an old man wearing a Welsh wig sitting on an obnoxiously high desk, causing his head to almost reach the ceiling.

"Fezziwig!" I shouted. "The best boss I ever had. I haven't thought about him in years."

When the enormous clock across the room struck 7 o'clock, it let out a loud "dong." Fezziwig looked up, put down his pen, and adjusted his waist coat as he belted out a jovial laugh.

"Ebenezer!" Fezziwig yelled. "Dick!"

I saw my former self, now a young man, scurry in with a fellow apprentice practically joined at my hip.

"That's Dick Wilkins," I said to the Ghost as I pointed toward the other apprentice. "Oh, I miss old Dick. Dick and I were so close back then. It's so good to see Dick again. I have such great memories of poor Dick."

***

An alert popped up on Dickens' screen, saying, "There are far too many cuss words in this paragraph. Please delete some cuss words before moving forward."

He scanned the paragraph repeatedly looking for the alleged offensive words. He decided to x out of the warning, which locked up his computer. An additional window popped up and said, "Admin password needed."

Dickens raised his hand to get The Supervisor's attention, who rolled his eyes, stood up, and walked over.

"What's the problem?" he asked.

"The machine is no longer working," Dickens said, pointing at the screen.

The Supervisor looked at the screen and typed in his password, which unlocked the computer. He read the last sentence and laughed out loud.

"What?" Dickens asked.

"Okay," The Supervisor said, trying to compose himself. "You have a character named Dick. You're gonna have to change that."

"What on earth is the reason for that?" Dickens asked, irritated.

"Well, the word 'dick' now, most of the time, means a man's genitalia," he said, smirking.

"Oh," he said. "The reader will think I'm referring to a penis?"

"Not really," he said, "But that's one of the words The Editor, and the software, will not tolerate. Just change the name to John, or whatever. Otherwise I'll be over here every two minutes unlocking your computer."

"I see," Dickens said, still confused. "I'll make the necessary adjustments."

"Good deal," The Supervisor said, slapping Dickens on the back.

As he walked away, Dickens mumbled to himself, "But my name is Dick-Ens. Would people think of genitalia when they say my name, too? Would they joke about 'Dick In?'"

He shrugged off that thought, as he went back to typing.

***

"My boys" Fezziwig said. "No more work for you tonight. It's Christmas Eve, ~~Dick~~ John. It's Christmas Eve, Ebenezer," he said, clapping his hands, so loudly it echoed throughout the building.

My younger self and ~~Dick~~ John ran outside in a fury and began closing shutters. We did so with such speed an onlooker would have thought we were trying to stop a fire, as opposed to trying to start a party. When we finished, we returned panting like dogs on a hot summer day.

Fezziwig maneuvered his large frame from where he was seated on the high desk, and with the agility of a gymnast, dismounted and ceremoniously stuck the landing.

I watched in awe as my former self and my former coworkers changed a place of business, which was adorned with the "warmness" of a warehouse, into a festive ballroom with the speed of stage hands changing sets between acts of a play.

There was a fiddler, lots of dancing, and an absurd amount of food. It appeared as if every person in the neighborhood attended, and I even noticed children known for begging in that neighborhood. All were invited, and all were welcome with a warm smile and a hug.

The Ghost and I watched on in delight. Feeling as if no time had passed, when the clock struck eleven, the party began to disperse. Fezziwig and his wife took their stations at either side of the door, shaking every hand, and wishing every face a Merry Christmas.

The room was mostly empty when it occurred to me I wasn't really at the party, my current self that is. I had forgotten about the Ghost and the previous scenes I'd witnessed that night. I saw my former self, along with ~~Dick~~ John, wish a Merry Christmas to the Fezziwigs, with a smile that can't be faked, a smile that isn't formed for someone else to see, a smile that's a manifestation of inner joy.

This hit me like a punch in the belly. I almost doubled over in the pain of loss: the loss of a part of myself that knew how to experience happiness.

I saw my former self turn down the lamps in the room, which was left in shambles from the party, and as the darkness fell, we were once again transported to another place.

"We must hurry," the Ghost said. "My time grows short."

A wintry, snowy setting faded up, and I saw my former, yet older, self. I was in the prime of my life, yet there was something different from the Ebenezer at Fezziwig's party. Less joy. More determination. Eager for different pursuits in life.

I wasn't alone. A beautiful young lady, Belle, was walking beside me, with pools of tears forming in her eyes.

"It is clear," she said, softly, "that I have been replaced."

"Replaced?"

"Yes," she said. "By another love."

"Who?" I asked.

"Not who," she said, "but what."

My previous self was interested, but not as interested as the conversation necessitated.

She continued, "Money."

My former self rolled his eyes, and said, "This is a cruel world, and there is nothing crueler than poverty. Nothing wards off poverty but the pursuit of wealth."

"You fear the world too much," she said, gently. "Greed will do nothing to calm those fears."

"So, you wish for me to be poor?" I asked.

She ignored my question, and said, "I have watched your noble traits wither away, over time, and I can no longer deny the few remaining noble traits will soon disappear, too."

"I've embraced reality," I retorted, curtly. "That has not changed how I feel about you."

She lowered her head, unable to look me in the eyes anymore, and said, "Ebenezer, I cannot say the same."

My previous self wasn't as stunned to hear those words as me, the current self, now helplessly witnessing the exchange. I hoped I would, or had, responded differently.

"We made promises," she said. "Since those promises were made, you have changed. When they were made, you were another man."

"I was not a man!" I said, nearly shouting. "I was a boy."

"Your response, right here, right now," she said, "proves you are, in fact, a different person. Since you are not the one who made those promises, I feel as if I should release you of them."

"Have I ever sought to be released from them?" I asked.

"In words?" she said. "No."

My former self shook his head, saying, "This is all very silly."

"I want nothing more than for it to be silly," she said, no longer in the soft, gentle tone. "It is truth. So, I release you to pursue your love."

She paused, choosing her words carefully, and said, "With a full heart, for the love of the man you once were, I release you."

My former self was about to speak, but she reached up with her hand to stop me.

"I do wish you happiness," she said. "You, the stranger standing before me, whom I do not know. May you find happiness and fulfillment in the life you have chosen."

She quickly walked away.

***

The steam whistle bellowed, pulling Dickens instantly out of his scene. Guards approached each cubicle. The Revisers carefully removed both their hair pieces, placing them on the desks next to their keyboards. Dickens did the same.

Other Revisers stood up with their hands in the air. Dickens remained seated until Guard 93 walked up.

"Mr. Dickens," he said. "Stand up and place your hands on the desk."

The guard gripped his rifle with one arm, and frisked Dickens with the other. It was an exceptionally personal frisking: a you-should-buy-a-guy-dinner-first frisking.

"Work day's over," Guard 93 said. "Time to get fed and put to bed."

After the frisking, he ordered Dickens to raise his hands above his head, and to join a line of Revisers forming toward the outer door of the Revision Room. Everyone was silent, so Dickens assumed talking was forbidden.

After a command to begin walking, the line of Revisers twisted its way out of the Revision Room, down a long corridor, and into a large cafeteria. On the way in, guards handed them cardboard boxes with the letters "K.F.C." on the side. Although no instructions were given, talking must have been forbidden in the cafeteria, as well.

The line of Revisers weaved around a series of long tables and took seats on metal chairs that felt as if they could collapse at any second. Everyone placed their boxes on the table in front of them and sat motionless. When all were seated, there were easily 200 people in the room. While in his cubicle, Dickens could only see a handful of Revisers, but, apparently, there were others located elsewhere in the Central Revision Complex.

Dickens looked down the line of seated Revisers, hoping to catch a glimpse of who they were, but after a mean look from a guard, he lowered his eyes to the table.

The door to the cafeteria slammed, as a guard shouted, "Bow your heads and close your eyes, Revisers."

Dickens' head was already bowed. He wanted to keep his eyes open — as he often did in church as a child, looking around to catch those whose eyes were also open, people who typically ended up being his friends — but Dickens had already been yelled at enough today. He closed his eyes just enough that they appeared closed. His eyelashes only slightly blurred his vision.

"Oh, God," screeched a man with a high-pitched voice. "We come before you today. Humbly. To sing your praises and worship you with our very lives. Please bless this food to the nourishment of our bodies. Let the food digest properly and provide us with much-needed energy. Once the food is digested, oh God, please let us never forget that you were the one who blessed us with this meal, on this day. May we remember it forever and ever …"

His stomach grumbled, as he wished this man would pray faster. He hadn't realized how hungry he was, having only eaten a few of the cheese-dusted chips on break, but now with the smell of food present, he felt ravenous. The sound of Dickens' stomach must have influenced other Revisers' stomachs, as he soon heard a symphony of complaining stomachs.

"… Oh, God," the man continued. "May we find new and innovative ways in which to worship you, and to bring glory to your name. Thank you, oh Lord, for the life of the chickens whom you gave life to, whom we will now use as energy to exalt you. And for the potatoes …"

The stomach complaints grew louder. If he didn't hurry up, the sounds of the growling stomachs might drown out the prayer of this shrill, long-winded man.

"… May we, oh Lord," he said, "never forget the sacrifice you paid for our sins. The debt we owe. The down payment on our eternal life. The holy nest egg of your son's sacrifice, who died upon a tree, after being whipped and tortured…"

Dickens felt this was torture, not just by the length of the prayer, but by the labored metaphors.

"… we, again, thank you," he said. "Oh, God. We thank you for this bounty. And with the kingdom, and the power, and glory, forever and ever, amen."

"Amen," roared the Revisers.

"Alright," a guard yelled. "Chow time."

They opened their boxes and began eating.

Inside the box was a flimsy bowl filled with mashed potatoes, corn, gravy, and chunks of chicken, all heaped together. Dickens removed the bowl and realized he had not received any cutlery. He looked around at his fellow diners, who were scooping the food out with their hands. He cringed at the thought, but, he was starving.

Dickens worked a finger into the bowl, scooped out a clump of food, and tasted it. It was good. He started scooping the food mush into his mouth like a starving animal. He wondered how he would get the sticky food off of his hands, but he was eating too ferociously to care. The sound of crumpling of boxes and bowls yielded to sounds of everyone sucking food remnants off their hands. Apparently, no hand-washing was needed. The other Revisers placed their bowls back into the boxes, closed them, and returned to sitting with their eyes directed toward the table.

The food was satisfying, but it hardly made a dent in his hunger. Could he go ask for more? He scratched that thought instantly. Something from his Birth Life, which he couldn't quite pinpoint, told him it was a terrible idea.

Who else was here? Any of his contemporaries? Any of his heroes? Even if he could look at the other Revisers, with everyone having shaved heads and faces, he might not recognize them. Despite the horribleness of the situation, being in this room, sitting among the most important writers of all time, was an honor. A very weird honor.

"Chow time's over!" yelled the guard.

Everyone stood up, grabbed their empty boxes, and filed out of the room, pitching their boxes in a trash bin next to the door. The Revisers filed out the doors and were directed down different hallways. Guard 93 guided Dickens, and those who worked near his cubicle, down a corridor labeled, "English Language Wing."

The hallway looked less like a prison, and more like a hotel. It was painted red, with gold-colored nameplates on each door. The guard stopped him in front of a room labeled, "Charles Dickens — English," and unlocked the door. After Dickens walked in, the door closed behind him with the nerve-racking metal crack of a jail cell.

During The Orientation, they mentioned a special room awaited him after his first day of work. They assured him he would feel right at home. He didn't feel at home. He didn't even want to look at the room. He merely slumped into a chair near the door. Dickens had dreaded this moment for hours. Now, his mind was his only companion. Under these circumstances, no roommate would be worse than his own mind.

His mind turned back to his family. Did they lead happy lives? How did they die? Did he even want to know how his children or grandchildren's lives unfolded? Maybe, he'd learn great things. Maybe, he'd learn awful things. Maybe, his descendants were proponents of the Modern Truth Movement.

He never thought about it before, but there was comfort in dying.

"I'm glad I'll never live to see the day," old-timers often say.

"Not in this lifetime," others proclaim.

The feeling of "Glad I'll never see the day," was pounding in his mind like a hammer. Especially since he DIDN'T live to see the day, but he, unfortunately, was still having to see it.

To occupy his mind, he decided to look around his special-made residence. A few feet past the door was a small bathroom. Nothing special about that. The only other room was a medium-sized sleeping area, with a bed in the middle and a smattering of furniture scattered along the walls.

On the walls hung a mess of framed photographs, all of which were of people he didn't know. One photo of a rather large man was labeled "Winston Churchill." Another, of a man in military uniform, was labeled "General Montgomery." The largest piece was a color photo of a man with long brown hair and his face half-painted blue, labeled "William Wallace."

"What?" he said, to himself. "Do they think I'm Scottish? And there's no way that's William Wallace."

But then he remembered it was entirely possible it WAS William Wallace, since he could have been Resurrected. Perhaps he lived in the room next door. He shrugged to himself and moved past the photo of Mel Gibson from "Braveheart."

A bookshelf crammed with books, most of which were Shakespeare, sat across from the bed. Not helpful. How many of these books were under Revision? Was Shakespeare making Iago the hero of Othello? Was Merchant of Venice now a guide to investing? Do Romeo and Juliet get saved right before they die, making it a happy ending?

He spotted a copy of "Sketches by Boz" crammed between "The Canterbury Tales" and "Gulliver's Travels". He removed it from the shelf, and let out a deep, cathartic laugh.

"I bet they have no idea I wrote this," he said, to himself while flipping through the pages. "Oh, this brings back some good memories."

His melancholy mood lifted momentarily, as he placed the book back on the shelf.

A large black rectangular item hung on the far wall. It was outlined with what looked like a window seal, rather than a picture frame. Clearly not a window. Clearly not a photograph. It looked like his computer monitor before it was turned on, which was the closest frame of reference he had for a 60-inch, flat-screen television.

A black chord with two metal prongs came out from the bottom of the item, near a small rectangular plate with four slots in it. It took him a second, but when he realized the prongs at the end of the cord were supposed to be pushed into slots on the wall, he plugged it in.

The black area in the middle came to life, revealing a live image of London. He took a step back to take it all in. Even though it wasn't the time period in which he lived, looking out upon the city did provide him a slight bit of comfort, followed by homesickness, that caused his mind to rage again. He reached down and unplugged the object, which once again turned to black.

He noticed a tapping coming from the bathroom. He ignored it at first as he continued to look around the room at various trinkets and knickknacks, assuming it was some sort of noise associated with modern plumbing.

As the tapping grew louder, he decided to check it out. He walked into the bathroom and sensed it was coming from underneath the sink. When he opened the doors to the cabinet, the sound grew even louder. He thumped the p-trap a few times to replicate the noise. It stopped. Then it started up again and began repeating five rhythmic beats over and over.

He stuck his head in the cabinet and noticed a folded-up piece of paper taped to the underside of the sink. Unfolding the paper, he saw what looked like a key to Morse Code, something that had been around in his Birth Life, but that he never needed to learn.

Dickens found a pencil in a desk, grabbed a copy of Romeo and Juliet, which had a few blank pages in the back, and headed into the bathroom to start writing down the message. He struggled at first to keep up, but finally was able to put together "S-C-H-E-N".

"What does that mean?" he mumbled.

He took his pencil and started tapping on the pipe himself, and immediately the other tapping stopped, as he slowly tapped out the letters "G-O-S-L-O-W-E-R".

The tapping started up again much slower. He recorded the letters "N-I-E-T-Z-S-C-H-E".

"S-C-H-E-N" … The last four letters of Nietzsche's last name and the first letter of his first. That seemed obvious now.

He needed to shake some of the cobwebs off his brain, so to speak, and that thought made him laugh, since he literally might have had that problem, having just been dead days ago.

Tired and loopy, he decided to test out Nietzsche's sense of humor, tapping out the message "G-E-R-M-A-N-P-E-O-P-L-E-S-T-I-N-K."

He laughed to himself, and eagerly waited for the philosopher's response to a childish insult.

After a moment of silence, Nietzsche's response was: "Y-O-U-R-M-O-T-H-E-R-I-S-W-O-R-M-F-O-O-D".

"My mother is worm food?" he thought. "Well, I suppose she is, but so was I until the other day."

Was this a playful insult? Or a real one? Or was he just stating a fact? Regardless, he decided to move on.

Dickens tapped out: "where are you?"

Nietzsche responded with: "my room. next door."

Dickens asked: "what are you doing?"

Nietzsche tapped back: "looking at a view of germany i don't recognize."

Dickens laughed loudly. It was comforting to know he wasn't the only one who found his room's décor confusing.

Dickens: "why the tapping?"

Nietzsche: "to talk"

Dickens: "about what?"

Nietzsche: "what do you think?"

Dickens: "being raised from the dead to revise books?"

Dickens was impressed with how much faster he was already getting with this code.

Nietzsche: "there is a resistance."

Dickens: "to put a stop to this?"

Nietzsche: "yes … america isn't all bad … we have friends."

Dickens thought about his first trip to America in his Birth Life. He had high hopes but wound up being severely let down. His second trip to America went much better, and he left with a better opinion of the country and those who inhabited it. He wondered if any of the American writers he met were Revising their books, too. If so, were they still mad at him for saying bad things about America?

Nietzsche: "i will tell you more about the resistance later … we shouldn't do this long …guards will catch on … we are being watched."

Dickens: "watched?"

Nietzsche: "our bathrooms are the only places not video recorded."

Dickens: "ok … thanks."

Nietzsche tapped back: "Y.W."

Dickens asked: "what?"

Nietzsche: "u r welcome … u need 2 learn abbrev … or this will take 4ever."

Dickens: "O.K."

Nietzsche: "u should know a few things … this isn't real morse code … memorize it and throw it away … never start tapping a message … i will begin when it's time … tomorrow you will have 1 more bible on your desk … always start the day with a bible verse … luke 16:13 … i also like Song of Solomon 2:3.

Dickens: "K"

Nietzsche: "i go now."

Dickens: "1 question?"

Nietzsche: "K. 1."

Dickens: "is this a dream?"

Nietzsche: "i wish."

Dickens: "nightmare?"

Nietzsche: "no … the abyss."

Dickens wasn't exactly sure what he meant, but he got the idea.

Dickens tapped: "thanks … goodnight."

Nietzsche tapped back: "YW. GN."

Dickens studied the code until he had it memorized and pitched it in the toilet. He ripped out the pages from Romeo and Juliet he'd used decoding messages, wadded them up, and flushed them down the toilet.

Back in the bedroom, he was very aware of being watched. He walked across the room in what he hoped was an innocent-looking way, returned the book, and started preparing for bed.

He felt better than he had at any point in his Resurrection Life. It was not a dream. It was certainly a nightmare. And, yes, the Abyss was a good way to describe it, but the thought of a Resistance made him smile … and gave him hope.

Dickens woke up the next morning to the sound of an alarm blasting from a speaker in the corner of his room. He tried to ignore it, but a voice from the speaker said, "Get up Mr. Dickens. Be ready for work in ten minutes."

He was dead tired, which seemed funny. "Dead Tired" was more appropriate than ever before. He tried to ignore the alarm, throwing his covers over his head. The voice said, "I see that, Mr. Dickens. You now have nine minutes."

He begrudgingly removed the covers and stepped out of bed. He disappeared into the bathroom, partially to avoid being watched, and to start getting ready. When he finished in the bathroom, a small tray was sitting next to his bed. On it sat a small cup of black coffee, a slice of butter, and a muffin-like item he didn't recognize. It was what Americans refer to as an "English muffin." Quickly, he smeared butter all over the English muffin and devoured it in only a few bites. The taste of the muffin was okay, but he wanted more.

How peculiar it was to eat dinner like a prisoner last night, and now he was getting room service? It was a humble room service, but still, the difference was jarring, and very confusing.

He and the other Revisers were back at their desks in the Revision Room a few minutes after waking up. Once the guards made sure Dickens took his seat and didn't have any problems getting his computer started, they resumed their posts at an entrance.

His hair pieces had been moved and looked neater than before. He picked up his mustache first, and before he had it in place, he noticed it smelled of some sort of cleaning fluid. His wig smelled the same. He supposed it was good that his fake wig and facial hair had been washed, but after a few moments the smell from his mustache grew nauseating.

Thinking of Nietzsche's words from last night, Dickens looked at the row of books on the shelves above his desk and, surely enough, a New Earth Translation Bible had been added. Trying to act casual, he reached up and grabbed the bible, and thumbed over to Luke 16:13. He read the verse, which ended in the phrase, "Man cannot serve two masters: God and wealth."

The following verse, Luke 16:14, looked a little odd. Instead of continuing with another bible verse, in the same typeface and same color of paper, it said "Use "U" instead of "You". "R" instead of "are" or "our". Use "gr8" instead of "great" … and so forth.

The entire rest of the column was filled with information like that, but the following column went back to scripture. It appeared to be some sort of sticker placed over the column and wasn't a part of the original printing of the book. Very clever, Dickens thought to himself.

He flipped to the other verse, which was Song of Solomon 2:3. It read, "As the apple tree among the trees of wood, so is my beloved among the sons. I sat down under his shadow with great delight, and his fruit was sweet to my taste."

The next verse read, "I hid the abbreviations underneath the other verse. You should start your day with a quick reading of that other bible verse, in case I needed to convey something that couldn't be tapped out easily in code. I chose the previous because it's one that I'm gathering no one around here would ever read. I chose this verse, just for today. This is a verse about oral sex. In the Christian bible. I think it's funny and thought it might help lift your mood. Hope it worked. Your friend, ..."

He wondered how Nietzsche got the messages into the bible. Maybe he'd find out as he learned more about The Resistance. He felt a sense of pride.

Proud to be part of The Resistance. Hopefully they could find a way to stop the Revisions projects. No. It HAD to be stopped.

In order to not attract too much attention, he decided to get started. He cracked his knuckles and looked over the original manuscript to find where he'd left off.

"Oh!" Dickens said to himself. "Belle had just dumped Scrooge as a young man, and he's about to see what he missed out on."

With the fresh day of writing ahead, he decided to add another chapter heading.

CHAPTER 2 ½: THE FIRST OF THE THREE SPIRITS … IS STILL BLATHERING

or
BELLE HAD A FUCK-TON OF KIDS

With a wave of his hand, the Ghost instantly transported us into a different time and place. We were in the family room of a modest house. It radiated warmth, making me feel welcome even though I wasn't really there.

I saw a young woman sitting by the fire whom I thought, upon first glance, was Belle, my former fiancé, but when I noticed the woman sitting across from her, I realized this was Belle, and there was no question the young lady was her daughter. Belle was older, but the years had been very, very kind. She beamed with a unique brand of joy I hadn't seen since we first met.

I'd been so focused on Belle, and her lookalike daughter, that I failed to notice that the room was exploding with children. The racket they generated would have agitated most people, but Belle looked at peace.

Someone knocked at the door, and a mob of children ran to open it. A man walked in carrying Christmas packages, stacked so high they obscured his identity. As he shuffled toward the tree, the herd of kids mauled him, each taking a present, proceeding to shake it, feel it, or smell it in efforts to identify the toy hidden inside.

Belle cheered as the children swarmed the man, thoroughly enjoying their rowdy behavior. When the man had shed the last of the presents, and the last of the children, he removed his coat and scarf and dropped onto the chair next to Belle. The man, who now we could identify as Belle's husband, feigned a look of annoyance at the children, but his smile revealed delight. The room was now silent, as the little ones appeared to have taken on the persona of Sherlock Holmes in "The Mystery of the Wrapped Present."

Belle and her husband exuded happiness, as they locked eyes, having one of those telepathic conversations longtime couples often have. Her husband's smile transformed from one of happiness to one more mischievous than a kid in detention.

"Belle," he asked. "Saw an old friend of yours this afternoon."

"Who?" she asked.

"Guess!"

"How can I know?" she added, realizing the previous times she'd seen this particular mischievous smile. They laughed and, in unison, said, "Mr. Scrooge!"

"Correct, my dear," the husband said. "I walked past his counting house and peeked through the window. All I saw was a lone candle lighting up his face."

"So sad," she said, but I couldn't tell if this was genuine or sarcastic.

"Such a lonely life, and it's about to get even lonelier," her husband said. "I hear old Marley's on his death bed."

"Oh, that's a shame about Marley," she said. "I wouldn't worry too much about Ebenezer, though."

"Why not?" her husband asked.

"Marley has no family or friends," she said. "I expect Mr. Scrooge will be twice as rich whenever Marley's gone."

"Right!" her husband said. "Scrooge might be the happiest mourner the undertaker's ever seen."

"He and his true love can finally be alone together," she said.

Belle and her husband burst into cackling, belly-laughs, which was the final straw for me.

"Spirit?" I said, trembling. "Please remove me from this place."

The Ghost nodded, agreeing I could take no more, and with that, I was instantly back in my bedroom.

The pain and frustration that had plagued me suddenly morphed into exhaustion. Realizing I was going to fall asleep whether I liked it or not, I used my remaining energy to stumble toward my bed, falling fast asleep.

***

Dickens stopped typing.

In his Birth Life, this scene was wonderful to write. It was based on his actual home life. Their home was happy at that time, and he admired his wife Catherine's ability to maintain a smile when their children acted rambunctious. It made her happier. Many mothers fumed when their kids weren't acting like little statues. Dickens and Catherine both believed harsh, unnecessary discipline squashed something within children. Something they could never get back.

But, then, it hit him:

"Oh, God! Catherine!" Dickens whispered to himself. "I left her."

Late in life, he abandoned her for a much younger woman, Ellen. His actions humiliated Catherine. The public demonized Ellen.

Guilt plagued him for the pain he'd caused both women, followed by loving thoughts about his time spent with both Catherine and Ellen, followed by the pain of missing them, and, again, followed by pangs of guilt.

Love. Guilt. Remorse. Love. Sadness. Homesickness. Love. Sorrow. Guilt. Shame. Loneliness.

Inundated with this spectrum of emotions, he fought to lose himself in his Revision. After several attempts, he accepted defeat. He had no choice but to ride out this mental hurricane, while still appearing busy.

He felt stupid doing it, but the only solution he found was typing out random phrases on his computer, pretending to ponder, and then delete them.

He typed, pondered, and deleted … typed, pondered, and deleted … typed, pondered, and deleted … up until break time. After which, he typed, pondered, and deleted … typed, pondered, and deleted … typed, pondered, and deleted … up until The Supervisor walked up to Dickens' desk, flanked by four guards.

"Mr. Dickens," The Supervisor said, "you have to report to The Doctor for a routine checkup. Please remove your hairpieces and stand up with your hands raised."

"Of course," Dickens said, delighted for the distraction. Any distraction.

With four rifles pointed at him, Dickens removed his beard and wig, raised his hands, and slowly stood up.

"Me and these guards are taking him for a checkup," The Supervisor yelled, to the other Revisers. "That doesn't mean y'all get to take a break."

After a long walk down a series of corridors, they stopped by a set of double doors fit with an elaborate security system. The Supervisor stepped aside, allowing Guard 93 to approach a security kiosk. He lowered his weapon and pushed his face toward a small, black screen. The security system began beeping, as a horizontal, red laser scanned the guard's face from top to bottom. The system emitted a loud, but friendly-sounding beep, as the doors unlocked with a clunk.

The Supervisor grabbed the handle and opened the door for Dickens and the guards, saying, "Mr. Dickens, the guards will take you the rest of the way."

He nodded toward The Supervisor, as he and the guards entered and walked down a hallway. Dickens' stomach turned, like it was being used to polish rocks.

An odor smacked him in the face: cleaning chemicals with a hint of rotting flesh. The guards also winced, a rare sign of humanity.

They stopped at a room, labeled "Resurrection Machine Room," with an even more elaborate security system. Guard 93 pressed a button on a kiosk, and a small television screen above the kiosk flickered to life. A young man's face appeared on the screen, and through an intercom, said, "Are you here with Mr. Dickens?"

"Yes," Guard 93 said, pressing the button while he spoke. "Is The Doctor ready?"

"He is," the man said. "I'll let you in."

The man's face disappeared from the screen, the system buzzed, and the door unlocked. The guards stepped back, and Dickens followed suit.

One of the doors opened and the man from the screen, wearing a long, white lab coat, held the door open as they filed into the room.

The room, framed with fluorescent lights that forced squinting, was large enough to house a fleet of elephants. Three additional young men, also wearing long lab coats, worked at computer stations near the room's entrance. None of them broke concentration from their work as Dickens and the guards entered.

At the opposite end of the room sat a massive computer station decked out with an array of buttons and switches and lights. Bundles of wires and cords, wrapped together with cable ties, fed out from the back and curled into a metal box, suspiciously the size of a coffin. Hoses snaked out of the box, coiling up the wall and along the floor, feeding into a hospital bed positioned toward the center of the room. The hoses, with their ends capped by needles, lined metal rails along both sides of the bed.

The setup looked both professional, and makeshift, as if a state-of-the-art machine were torn apart and reassembled in a tinkerer's basement.

A man, also wearing a lab coat, sat with his back to the door at the opposite end of the room beside the large computer station. The other men in the room were young and clean cut, whereas, this man's shoulder-length gray hair curled wildly in every direction.

The young man walked them over to the gray-haired man, and said, "Doctor, the Dickens unit is here to see you."

The man removed a pen from his pocket, clicked it, took down a note, swiveled his chair around, and slowly stood up.

The Doctor's hair covered his face like a slightly parted set of drapes. He had a scraggly beard, with hairless spots that revealed deep acne scars. The white lab coat he wore contrasted with his seemingly artificial tan. His appearance, for some reason, made Dickens expect an Eastern-European accent, but when he spoke, he had a slow, but calculating, American accent.

"Charles Dickens," The Doctor said. "You don't remember me, do you?"

Dickens shook his head.

"That's okay," he said. "You were freshly Resurrected. Most Revisers don't remember the first day of their Resurrection Life."

"Yes," he said. "I don't remember much before The Orientation."

"Well," he said. "You and I had quite a chat. You were convinced I was God."

Dickens had zero recollection of this.

"Which," he said, "is flattering, but just because I Resurrect people doesn't make me God."

The Doctor laughed with a loud, exaggerated cackle, as if trying to sound evil.

Gesturing toward the Machine, The Doctor said, "Truthfully, I didn't even invent the Resurrection Machine, but I am the one who made it glorify God. The real God, not me."

He cackled again, and even the guards seemed uneasy.

"But we should get around to why you are here," he said, motioning toward a piece of furniture that looked like a massage chair. Dickens stepped up to it, but stopped, unsure of how to he was supposed to sit.

The Doctor patted the seat, and said, "Sit down right here, Mr. Dickens," and pointing to the upper part, he said, "and your face goes here."

He worked his way onto the chair and lowered his face into the headrest.

"Thank you, Mr. Dickens," The Doctor said, as he snapped on a pair of latex gloves. "This should only take a minute."

The headrest on the chair obscured Dickens' peripheral vision, preventing him from seeing anything but the shiny, linoleum floor, the color of which should be named "hospital gray." He opted to view the inside of his eyelids. This lack of vision made the sounds clearer: the shuffle of The Doctor's footsteps, the clank of mysterious metal tools, the squeak of springs as The Doctor plopped on a chair, and the spinning of casters along the floor as he crept closer.

Dickens felt cold hands on the back of his head, causing him to jump.

The Doctor chuckled, and said, "Relax, Mr. Dickens."

"I'll try," he said, his voice muffled from the headrest.

"You know?" The Doctor said, now pushing on various spots on the back of Dickens' skull. "In one way, I feel sorry for you Revisers."

A long pause indicated that The Doctor wished for him to enquire, so he reluctantly asked, "Oh, how so?"

"The hair and beards, of course," he said, as if obvious. "I'd be lost without my hair and beard. It's the secret to my strength. You know? Like Sampson."

Dickens once again felt the tug of a conversation in which he did not want to participate, but since he didn't have a choice, he said, "Oh, yes. That strong bloke from the bible."

"Of course," The Doctor said. "I'm the one who convinced The Editor to let Revisers wear wigs. So, you can thank me for that."

He was fishing for gratitude about the beards and wigs. This time Dickens couldn't force a response. The wigs and beards were stupid, and for someone to use their influence for that, when real suffering was happening, was insulting.

The Doctor stopped the examination, and Dickens could sense no movement. He must have been sitting there, staring at the back of his head, waiting for gratitude for the wigs. After Dickens realized this was never going to stop until he responded, he rolled his eyes, even though the headrest obscured his face.

"I suppose I should thank you," Dickens said, begrudgingly. "I don't know why our heads and faces are shaved in the first place."

"Well, you're welcome," The Doctor said. "But the heads really aren't shaved. The hair has been permanently removed with a laser. I know your Birth Life was before the time of lasers, so I'll just say, it's a highly technical way of removing hair. There's this port on the back of your head that's created in the Resurrection process, which is what I'm running tests on right now. We keep the heads hair-free because it's easier for maintenance, and essential if we ever have to reconnect you to The Machine. As for the beards and mustaches, I do that because you'd look weird with no hair on your head but hair on your face."

"That's understandable," Dickens said. "I wouldn't mind hearing more about the Resurrection Machine."

"Um," The Doctor said, pausing his examination. "It's hard to explain. Lots of technical jargon and whatnot."

"I see," he said, disappointed. "Is there anything I would understand?"

"Yeah," The Doctor said, resuming the examination. "If you saw the back of your head right now, you'd probably pass out."

He laughed loud and hard. Dickens chuckled along, nervously.

"And that's the truth," The Doctor said, through his laughter. "There's not a whole lot I can tell you. It's hard to explain. Jargon and technical stuff you'd never understand."

"Very well," Dickens said.

"I mean, I CAN tell you that you have a microchip in the back of your skull, which I'm about to sew shut," he said. "But I'd have to explain to you what a microchip was first, right?"

"Correct," he said, with a fake chuckle. "I have never heard of a microchip."

"It's pretty advanced technology," The Doctor said. "The whole Resurrection process is hard to explain. Especially the Refleshification process. That's where we take bones and put flesh back on them. Or the Neuro-Defibrillators. That's also hard to explain. And the Coronary Metronome. Don't even get me started on how difficult it would be to explain that. You know?"

"Right," Dickens said. "Could you explain to me what the microchips do?"

"Ummmm," The Doctor said. "If you promise not to tell anyone, I'll tell you the microchip is part of the system called the Kill Switch."

"What is the Kill Switch?" Dickens asked.

"It's a switch on the Machine that would instantly kill everyone it's ever Resurrected," he said. "In case of an emergency. You know? If a situation got dangerous. You know?"

"I do know," he said, placating. "I appreciate you trusting me with such sensitive information."

"Yeah, well," he said. "I think I've said enough, and I'm pretty much finished with your examination."

"Thank you very much," Dickens said, sitting up in his chair to look at The Doctor. "May I ask who did invent the Machine?"

"Sure," The Doctor said, excitedly. "My mentor, Dr. Alex Wilderman. A pretty famous scientist. Nobel Prize winner. A McCarthy Genius, and all that. Smartest person I've ever met. Showed me all the ropes with the Machine and all of that. An atheist, unfortunately, but other than that, the best mentor I could have ever asked for."

"Was?" he asked. "Dr. Wilderman died?"

"Uh," The Doctor said, uncomfortable. "You know … I think we need to get you back to the Revision Room. Shouldn't hold up the Revising. That's why you're here, right?"

"Of course," Dickens said. "Thank you for your time."

"You're welcome," he said. "You know? I like talking to you. You're nothing like that smart-ass Nietzsche."

A few minutes later, Dickens returned to the Revision Room. He couldn't wait for the end of his shift, so he could ask Nietzsche all about The Doctor. He wondered what Nietzsche did to make him unhappy. He imagined one of the greatest minds of the 19th Century had drawn the same conclusion as Dickens: That The Doctor knew nothing about The Machine he was operating, and the chance that he was an actual doctor was nil.

His amusement and intrigue about The Doctor subsided quickly, as his mind returned to the depressing thoughts about Catherine and Ellen. He returned to his time-wasting tactic.

He typed, pondered, and deleted … typed, pondered, and deleted … typed, pondered, and deleted … until the work day was over.

After dinner, which was the same K.F.C. bowl, the guards walked Dickens back to his room, and, once inside, he managed to push the dreadful thoughts about his family out of his mind. He eagerly waited to communicate with

Nietzsche. Too antsy to focus on anything, but, not wanting to raise suspicion from the people watching him, he plugged in the TV with the view of London. He grabbed a random book from the bookshelf, took it to the bed, and pretended to read while he waited.

After about an hour, he heard the tapping again from the bathroom. He calmly got up and, while still pretending to read, walked into the bathroom and shut the door.

He squatted on the floor and opened the cabinet. He flipped to the back of the book he'd pretended to read to find a few blank pages, got out his pencil, and started to write.

The message was just the word "Hi," over and over again.

"Hi. Hi. Hi. Hi. Hi. Hi. Hi. Hi. Hi. Hi. Hi. Hi. Hi. Hi. Hi."

Dickens tapped: "Hi," in return.

Nietzsche tapped: "we r trying 2 end this … we hav help but cant say who … cant say how i got messages n ur bible … some1 who is being very helpful could get hurt."

Dickens was relieved a little. He could understand most of this conversation, even though he didn't learn the abbreviations as well as planned. He might have to look over what he'd written down, once they were finished.

Dickens: "k"

Nietzsche: "plan: we r trying 2 gather info on how the crc works … in the meantime, we also r trying 2 get info on the outside world … feeding us info is 2 risky … it is 4 bidden … whatever u can gather from overhearing guards, etc … make note."

Dickens: "k"

Nietzsche: "there r 5 newspapers stashed n shakespeares room … its ben r best source of info on the outside world … but its all ben cut off."

Dickens: "y?"

Nietzsche: "a college kid worked here 4 a while … he was n an english class and philosophy 2 … shakes and i wrote a couple of papers 4 him n exchange 4 newspapers."

Dickens: "y no more newspapers?"

Nietzsche: "prof gave us bad grades."

Dickens erupted in laughter. Professors in the United States received a philosophy paper written by Fredrich Nietzsche, and an English paper written by William Fucking Shakespeare, and they both wound up giving them bad grades. He couldn't remember, in this life or the first, hearing something as perfect as that.

Dickens: "ha"

Nietzsche: "the philosophy profs comments were insane."

Dickens: "ha"

Nietzsche: "use l.o.l. … not ha"

Dickens: "k"

Dickens wondered why, since typing out "ha" used fewer letters than "l.o.l.," whatever the fuck that meant.

Nietzsche: "college kid quit … now we have no source of info … but we have scrapbook … i will try 2 get it 2 u … 4 now, do your work … try not 2 look suspicious … k?"

Dickens: "k"

Nietzsche: "i will try 2 send u messages every night … let me know if u learn anything new."

Dickens: "k"

Nietzsche: "need 2 go. gn"

Dickens had important questions to ask, beyond his curiosity about The Doctor. He frantically tried to figure out a way to type out a complicated question with an abbreviation.

Dickens: "1quest un"

He hoped that made sense. He was more or less making up those abbreviations on the fly.

Nietzsche: "no time"

Dickens whispered, "Fuck!" to himself, and was about to tap "GN," to wish Nietzsche a goodnight, but stopped himself. He sensed Nietzsche's urgency, and knew he shouldn't do anything stupid.

While still on the floor, he looked over the notes to make sure he understood everything. The members of The Resistance are trying to gather information about the outside world, and gather information about the inner works of the "CRC." (Dickens couldn't remember what that stood for. He just knew it was written on the back of his jumpsuit.) We have friends, but they are vulnerable. We need to do what they ask us to do, and try not to make anyone suspicious.

Once he had the message figured out, he ripped the pages out of the book, tore them into tiny pieces, and flushed them down the toilet. He hoisted himself up off the bathroom floor, trudged into the bedroom, and plopped on the bed.

He felt physically wrecked from the emotions of the day. His head throbbed, his neck and shoulders ached. His stomach felt awful, plagued with both the queasiness of a meal not sitting right, and also with hunger. He was so famished, he wished he'd chewed up and swallowed the pages he'd flushed down the toilet.

Nevertheless, just like the night before, messaging with Nietzsche gave him hope. Not much hope, but enough to get him through another day. With any luck, he could grow even more hopeful after a full conversation with Nietzsche.

Or Shakespeare! Holy shit! William Shakespeare was here. No doubt, working at a nearby cubicle and living a few doors down.

Dickens wondered why Nietzsche lived next door, if this is an English-speaking area. Obviously, he speaks English, but shouldn't he live with German speakers? He decided to ask Nietzsche about that whenever he got the chance.

He closed his eyes, attempting sleep, but his mind was now occupied with another thought. Thankfully, it was a fairly pleasant thought.

He mulled over the idea of writing a story about all of this. About what a man would think of his life if he woke up 150 years later, after all of his loved ones had died. He almost jumped out of bed to take notes, but before he did, he realized this was silly. Even if there were a way to write this novel and get it published, what are the odds that none of the other Revisers, the greatest writers of all time, hadn't thought to write something based on this experience?

The thought of others churning out brilliant plays, novels, and philosophical texts somehow made him feel better. He should consider writing a novel about this experience, but he would have to find a way to present his own unique perspective. As he often did in his Birth Life, he noted the idea's potential, and would let it twirl around in the back of his mind.

Seconds later, Dickens drifted off to sleep, worn out from what had been an unbelievably bizarre, and stressful day.

After eating his morning English muffin, Dickens was escorted into the Revision Room. He started the computer, and, unlike yesterday, actually found himself somewhat eager to write. Hopefully that would keep him from feeling depressed.

After a moment, Nietzsche whispered, "Charles, don't forget to start your day with scripture."

"Oh!" Dickens whispered. "I forgot. Thanks!"

He grabbed the New Earth Translation Bible and turned to Luke 16:13. The messages from the day before were gone, replaced with different text.

"CD, I had to tell FN last night to keep your chat short. A plumber was unclogging toilets for a couple of Russian writers. The Russians are always clogging up their toilets. I'm not sure why, since they are eating the same food. Whenever anything in the CRC is out of the ordinary, we've learned it's best to proceed with caution. I don't anticipate anything like that this evening, so I think you can have a long chat. I'm glad you're with us. To show my appreciation for helping our cause, I slipped some alcohol into your room. I hope you like vodka. On the back of your bathroom sink, there are a couple bottles. Lotion. Shampoo. Mouthwash, etc. The mouthwash bottle is vodka. I know things here are tough, so hopefully this will help. Don't let FN know. He's not a fan of alcohol. One time I had to break up a fight between FN and Hemingway, when they were just talking about alcohol."

Dickens almost laughed out loud but managed to suppress it in time.

The note continued: "Just keep writing. Don't attract suspicion. Help is on the way! Sincerely, The Insider."

This put Dickens in a good mood. He wasn't sure if he was happier about the promise of help or the alcohol awaiting him at the end of the day. It didn't matter. He road this wave of optimism as he began Revising, deciding to a have a little fun with the next scene: the scene when Scrooge meets the Ghost of Christmas Present.

CHAPTER 3: THE SECOND OF THE THREE SPIRITS

or
THE GHOST THAT'S KIND OF A HIPPIE

I expelled an extraordinarily loud snore, jolting me out of my catatonic slumber. As consciousness rushed upon me, a montage of my supernatural experiences replayed in my mind. The Marley-faced doorknocker. Marley's Ghost. Ghost of Christmas Past. I questioned whether it was all a dream, just as I heard a loud, jovial voice boom from the next room. It called my name to come join him, so I wiped some sleep out of the corners of my eyes and obeyed the Ghost's command.

After I slowly opened the door, I saw the room was extravagantly redecorated. It looked like a garden devoted to Christmas plants, holly, mistletoe, and ivy, and, on the floor, was a Christmas dinner feast fit for a king — or more like 2 or 3 kings — for the food was piled all the way up to the ceiling. Turkey, dressing, plum-pudding, chestnuts, apples, oranges, pears, fruit cake, and a steaming bowl of punch. Sitting upon the food pile, as if it were his thrown, was a jolly, glorious, giant man.

"Come in!" exclaimed the Ghost. "Come in and know me better, man."

***

Dickens read that last line and tried to think of a way to rephrase it to fit modern language. "Come in and let's get to know one another," he mumbled to himself, thought about it for a second, and decided it would be a suitable change.

He attempted to type in the updated line, but it quickly auto-filled the line "Come in and know me better, man." He attempted to delete the line, but it wouldn't let him. He was still able to type and could delete other phrases, but he was unable to delete that one line.

Dickens raised his hand, and The Supervisor, looking hungover this morning, walked over.

"Sir," Dickens said, "I am trying to modernize this line, but it won't let me change it. Or delete it."

The Supervisor leaned in and right-clicked on the phrase, and up popped a dialogue box, stating: "This phrase is too memorable, and has been flagged as 'Don't Change'."

"Okay," The Supervisor said, confused. "That's a phrase, I guess, that's too popular to change."

"Too popular?" Dickens asked.

"Uh, I guess it must be," he said, pointing toward the screen. "We aren't supposed to change phrases that are too well known. Otherwise, people might notice it's a Revision."

"Soooo," Dickens said, baffled. "I'm changing the entire text of this book, including very important plot points, but readers won't notice as long as I leave in this sentence?"

"Somebody thinks so," The Supervisor said. "It's like when Shakespeare Revised Hamlet. We weren't supposed to change, 'To be or not to be'. People who've never even heard of Hamlet know that line. I'd even heard of it."

"How could they not notice an entire book was Revised?" Dickens said. "Are modern people really that stup…"

He stopped talking mid-word. Nothing good could come from him completing this sentence, especially since he wasn't supposed to raise suspicion.

The Supervisor gave him a stern look that said, "Tread carefully." A look that, apparently, transcended generations.

After a long silence, The Supervisor said, "If you don't agree, you'll have to take that up with The Overseer, or maybe even The Editor himself."

He smirked, and added, "They LOVE hearing criticism."

Dickens understood the tone of this sentence too. Sarcastic, with a hint of "I dare you."

"I understand," Dickens said, nodding. "Thank you for the clarification."

He turned back to his computer and resumed typing, as The Supervisor walked away with an air of victory.

***

"I am the Ghost of Christmas Present!"

The Ghost's robe was tied loosely, allowing his broad, hairy chest to poke through. His coarse chest hairs looked like plants, bending out from beneath cover to reach sunlight. His feet were bare, and his head was wrapped with a holly wreath. His dark-brown hair was long and curly.

"You have never seen me before?" the Ghost said.

"Never," I said, my voice unsteady.

"Have you met any of my elder brothers?" the Ghost asked.

"Not that I know of," I said, confused. "Do you have many brothers?"

"More than eighteen hundred," said the Ghost, laughing cheerfully.

"Big family," I said, impressed. "It must be expensive to provide for such a family."

I felt silly, after I said that. I was talking to a Ghost, and it's unlikely they live within the financial constraints of humans.

"Ghost," I said, changing the subject. "Take me where you wish, for I am certain you have much to teach me."

"Touch my robe," the Ghost said.

I reached up and grabbed a handful. Instantly, we were standing in the city streets on Christmas morning. The weather was not pleasant. The sky was gray, heaps of soot-covered snow lay on every roof, and the streets were muddy. Despite the weather, everyone, adult and children alike, went about their business with a cheerfulness not found even on the sunniest day of summer.

Most patrons were in good spirits, but on an occasion, when the Ghost spotted someone who looked frazzled, he would raise his torch and sprinkle incense on their heads. After a few drops, their holiday spirit was restored.

"Are you spreading good cheer to anyone in particular?" I asked.

"This cheer is offered to anyone," he said, "but especially to the poor."

"Why the poor?" I asked.

"Because the poor need it the most," he said.

"Hmmm," I said, with curiosity. "Spirit, I am wondering why you, caring so deeply about the poor, deprive them of the ability to dine with their families every seventh day?"

"I do that?" the Ghost asked. "What the fuck are you talking about?"

"You want to close these places on the Seventh Day," I said. "Forgive me if I'm wrong, but it seems to be done in your name, or that of your family."

"There are some upon this earth of yours," said the Ghost, "who pretend to know us, and who do their deeds of hatred, envy, bigotry, and selfishness in our name. They are strangers to us, and their actions are their own."

**

Dickens stopped to think about this last exchange between Scrooge and the Ghost. It referred to something specific to the time period. Something a modern reader wouldn't understand. It could still be relevant, he thought, since modern leaders from what he'd seen were religious … and corrupt. The abuses of one man to another was bad enough, but when the abuser claims those actions were God's will, it can be catastrophic.

Were modern people forced to go to church, as had been attempted in his day? Were poor people still treated as deserving of their poverty, due to judgment from a deity? Maybe worse atrocities were done in the name of religion? Things beyond his imagination.

He looked up at his reference shelves and saw three books he had yet to open, titled: "God's Prosperity Promise" and "Blessed or Oppressed?" and "Poor No More!!!" all of which were written by someone named Kenneth Rich. He selected them, one at a time, and flipped through them. It was amusing how similar the books were, as if they were the same book with the chapters rearranged.

All three books had the same myopic message that God wanted you to be rich, not poor. The books didn't, however, have much to say about sin, judgment, or God's wrath. In fact, the overall tone of the book was happy. Chipper, even. He never liked the depiction of an angry God, but this version of God made him uncomfortable, too.

As he placed the books back on the shelf and turned back to the writing, it occurred to him that the above passage, where he had taken a clear jab at religious authority, wasn't flagged by the software. When he skimmed back over it, he realized why. It was worded in a way that wouldn't jump out as a critique on religion, if someone did not understand the context. Furthermore, in the original version, he had intentionally lumped the three ghosts in as part of a collective deity, so to speak, since a direct critique of the God worshipped by the Church of England would have constituted blasphemy. Criticism directed toward Ghosts, even if they were, in this instance, used as a substitute, could never be considered blasphemous.

Could he do this again? Maybe offer criticism of the religious leaders of today, but fool those who oversaw the Revision process into thinking it was a comment about the Ghosts? He loved this idea, and started typing, deleting, and retyping revisions of the above phrase to offer a critique of modern religion. It was a task that proved itself to be trickier than he'd expected, since he didn't have much more to work with than what he'd gathered from flipping through the reference books.

The task wound up consuming his entire day, and as the steam whistle blew, indicating the end of the work day, he was relieved. He was eager to discuss all of this with Nietzsche. Also, he was starving, and was, surprisingly, acquiring a taste for the nightly K.F.C. bowl.

Back in his room, almost instantly, he heard the tapping coming from the bathroom. He grabbed scrap paper, a pen, and ran to take notes.

Nietzsche: "what did u want 2 ask last night?"

Dickens couldn't remember the exact question he wanted to ask, but he knew it was about family. His head wanted to ask about religion, but his heart wouldn't let him. He decided to ask an unrelated question:

Dickens: "how long have u been here?"

Nietzsche: "idk … I was 1 of the first brought back 2 life … details r blurry … i started n the german sector … but was moved 2 the english sector … when they moved Darwin."

That explains why Nietzsche was in his sector, which he was mildly curious about, but his heart was about to sneak in a question:

Dickens: "have u learned anything about your family?"

There was a long pause between taps. So long that Dickens wondered if that was the end of the conversation for the evening. Finally, Nietzsche answered.

Nietzsche: "yes."

Dickens: "gr8!"

Nietzsche: "not gr8."

Dickens: "y?"

Nietzsche: "i'd rather not."

Dickens: "i want 2 know about my children … my wife … my …"

Dickens stopped tapping to think about what exactly Ellen was to him. Mistress? Lover? Actress he hired for a play, and slept with for the rest of his life? But while he contemplated, Nietzsche started up again.

Nietzsche: "at best they r all dead. at worst …"

Again, there was a long pause.

Dickens: "yes? At worst?"

Nietzsche: "what if your work was used to justify the murder of millions of people?"

Dickens didn't know how to respond. Was he serious? Was he joking? Was he inventing a worst-case scenario?

Dickens: "joking?"

Nietzsche: "no."

Dickens: "jesus!"

Nietzsche: "i can't believe i trusted my sister … i can't talk about this anymore."

Dickens: "k"

Dickens thought about whether it was possible for his novels to have been used for some sort of evil purpose. He couldn't imagine how, but he knew, in the hands of dishonest people, it doesn't take much to justify evil.

Dickens: "i'm sorry."

Nietzsche: "trust me … u don't want 2 know … but i haven't heard anything about your family … or your works being used for bad reasons … but several here have discovered that … me … marx … adam smith … the intentions behind your writing doesn't matter … especially once u r dead."

Dickens: "i see."

Nietzsche: "in fact … don't even look up your own death … i went insane 4 the last decade of my life … my sister used my catatonic body 2 entertain guests."

Dickens: "i won't look up anything."

Nietzsche: "wish i never had … we have chatted enough … we should say GN"

Dickens: "GN"

Dickens tapped those last two letters in a way he hoped would communicate sympathy, which was silly. How could tapping convey sympathy?

Dickens hoisted himself off the floor, and then saw the bottle of mouthwash on the back of the sink, which he'd forgotten was vodka. He quickly grabbed it and chugged it. It burned all the way down his throat and into his stomach.

He waddled into the bedroom and lay down on the bed. He was so grateful he'd had access to alcohol, because if not, Nietzsche's story would have no doubt kept him up for the rest of the night. But shortly after Dickens stripped off his clothes and got under the covers, a warmness, from the alcohol came over him, and he found himself drifting off to sleep.

The next morning, Dickens sat at his desk, and, although he badly wanted to whisper some words of comfort to Nietzsche, he knew it was inappropriate to start up during their occasional inter-desk whispers. That conversation needed time to do it justice, so to speak, and the nighttime tapping would be more fitting.

Nietzsche had stopped their conversation so abruptly the night before, they didn't have a chance to discuss whether there would be anything in the scriptures this morning, but Dickens decided to check anyway. He grabbed the New Earth Translation Bible and turned to Luke 16:13.

"FN seemed distressed last night. He didn't want to talk, so I'm assuming he was reminded of the actions of his sister. I'm assuming you had inquired, as every Reviser does sooner or later, about the wellbeing of your family. As FN discovered, it is never a good idea to find out answers to these questions. But I took the liberty of looking up what happened to your children and, for your peace of mind, I'll give you a few details …"

Dickens closed the book. Did he really want to know? He'd thought he did, but what if it's horrible? He tried to will himself to place the book back on the shelf, but almost as if his hands weren't giving him a choice, he opened the book and continued to read.

"… Only a few details. I probably wouldn't be giving you any details, if I wouldn't have found only good news …"

A wave of happiness swept over Dickens that made his chest hot and his head hum.

"… All I will tell you is, the children who lived after your death all seemed to live good lives. As for other loved ones, I'll spare details, but, again, I didn't find anything exceptionally bad …"

This gnawed at Dickens, as he desperately wanted to know more, but he knew it was for the best.

"… Also, don't worry about FN. He's gone through hell since he learned about this, but I'm not exaggerating when I say, the man loves suffering. It sounds strange, but I think he's at his happiest while he's suffering. I hope you have a lovely day destroying your classic work of literature. —The Insider."

Dickens chuckled at this last line, closed the book, and placed it back on his shelf.

A weight had been lifted. Not just about his family, but about Nietzsche. He knew it was meant as a joke, but he actually thought he might enjoy destroying his classic work today, and he had a fun idea for how to start that:

PART 2: THE COMPLETELY SUPERFLUOUS BREAK IN THE MIDDLE

or
THERE WASN'T EVEN A PART 1.
HOW FUCKED IS IT THAT THERE'S A PART 2?

or
SERIOUSLY, PART 2 BEGINS IN THE MIDDLE OF A
FUCKING SCENE

The Ghost of Christmas Present and I, after traversing a maze of nonsensically laid-out streets, arrived at the doorstep of a pathetic little home owned by, none other than my clerk, Bob Cratchit. Before we walked in, the Ghost sprinkled a Christmas blessing on the threshold.

Inside, I saw Bob's homely wife, Mrs. Cratchit, but I could never remember that goofy woman's name. She and her second-eldest daughter were attempting to unfold a tablecloth, while the eldest son tried to place food on the table before the cloth was situated, drawing amused looks from both the mother and her daughter, which was weird because that would have pissed me off.

Two smaller children, a boy and a girl, bolted through the front door talking way too quickly to understand. It was something about having smelled items at a bakery and witnessing an enormous goose in the butcher's window. All were dressed in the nicest outfit they owned, which depressed the fuck out of me since, none of it was even remotely "nice".

"Where on earth is your father and Tiny Tim?" Mrs. Cratchit said, to no one in particular. "And Martha, too?"

"There's Martha, mother" shouted another girl, who appeared out of nowhere.

She pointed to the front window as the Cratchit's eldest daughter walked past.

"There's Martha, mother!" the two youngest Cratchits echoed. As soon as Martha walked through the door, they yelled, "Martha! Have you seen the goose?"

"Why bless your heart, my dear," Mrs. Cratchit said to Martha. "Why are you so late?"

"There's father!" cried the two youngest Cratchits, who were everywhere at once. "Hide, Martha, hide!"

Martha ducked into a closet before the front door opened. I rolled my eyes at the stupid ruse, but after a disapproving look from the Ghost, I composed myself.

Bob walked in wearing the shabby clothing he wore every day, but the clothes were brushed and ironed. Atop his shoulders sat his son, Tiny Tim, who held a little crutch and had his limbs supported by an iron frame.

"Where's Martha?" Bob asked.

"Not coming," Mrs. Cratchit said.

"Not coming?" Bob asked, disappointed. "On Christmas Day?"

Martha emerged from the closet prematurely, apparently not fully committed to the ruse. Hearing the closet open, Bob looked around and saw Martha, whose emergence dissolved his disappointment.

Bob lowered Tiny Tim down to the floor, with the help of Tim's younger, yet taller, siblings. Martha ran into Bob's arms.

"And how did Tiny Tim behave?" Mrs. Cratchit asked Bob.

"Brilliant," Bob said. "On our way home, he told me he hoped more people would see him in church, as it would be a nice reminder, on Christmas Day, about who made the lame walk, and blind men see, since he is a cripple."

***

Dickens scrutinized the previous paragraph.

Tiny Tim was a cripple, but what exactly was wrong with him? Dickens couldn't remember. He's short for his age and uses a crutch. But he's terminally ill, too? In the next stave, the Ghost of Christmas Future shows Scrooge the scene at the Cratchit house after Tiny Tim's death. What did he have in mind when he created this character?

He grabbed the generic dictionary from his shelf, hoping to find information about cripples to jar his memory. He looked up the word "Cripple" and it said, "A person who is physically disabled; most often who has the inability to walk or to walk without assistance. Considered offensive: Person with a Physical Disability, preferred."

"Oh, no!" he said to himself. "That wasn't an offensive term during my Birth Life, but I don't want to offend any modern cripples … or, uh, physically disabled … people."

Dickens moved his curser up to the word "cripple," hit delete, and immediately a warning box popped up on the screen, saying "Political Correctness Alert! Computer will be locked until further notice."

The Supervisor came running over, and when he saw the box on the computer, he bent over with a painful wince.

"What did you do?" The Supervisor asked.

"Nothing!" Dickens said. "I was changing the word cripple to a less offensive term."

"Nothing?" he yelled, as his face grew red. "You think that's nothing?"

An alarm began blaring throughout the Revision Complex. The other Revisers slowly raised their hands. Dickens, clueless about what was happening, slowly raised his hands, too. Guard 93 began marching up and down the rows of cubicles, looking at each computer screen. He stopped at Dickens' cubicle, leaned in to take a closer look at the screen, and motioned for The Supervisor to step aside. Six other guards walked over to the cubicle, guns drawn.

"G-93, I've located the seven-eighty-five," Guard 93 said, as he pressed his index finger to his ear. "My twenty is room Echo-Romeo-Romeo-Three. Suspect is Dickens, Charles Dickens. Area is secured."

The Supervisor began pacing as he talked to himself, oscillating back and forth between muttering and shouting.

"It's okay. It will be okay. These things happen … STUPID COCKSUCKING LITERARY PIECE OF SHIT!!! … This can be fixed … maybe it's not a big … FUCKING BRITISH CRUMPET EATING SACK OF … They won't fire you. You don't have enough strikes against … FOREIGN. HEATHEN. WASTE. OF. FUCKING. SPACE."

The Overseer, and a bunch of people Dickens didn't recognize, rushed into the office. They stopped next to The Supervisor, whose meltdown was still in progress, with concern and perhaps a hint of amusement.

The alarm stopped abruptly.

"What happened?" The Overseer shouted to no one in particular.

Noticing the guards were hovering around Dickens' desk, he and the others who'd rushed in, cautiously walked over. The guards parted as they stepped through. The Overseer gestured to the guards to resume their posts. Craning his neck into the cubicle, he took a long look at the alert on the monitor.

"What?" The Overseer said to himself, as his eyes grew wide open. "Oh, shit … pardon my French."

"I don't understand," Dickens said.

"That wasn't really French, dumbass," he said.

"Not that," Dickens said. "What did I do?"

The Overseer stared at him as if his question were asked in Swahili, and let out a condescending, one-syllable laugh.

Whispering into Dickens' ear, he said, "The Editor will explain what you did."

A few minutes later, he was tossed into the back of a van along with The Supervisor, who continued his curse-filled tirade. It was Dickens' first ride in an automobile, and it might have been exciting if it weren't for the black bag thrown over his head. Discomfort also hindered the experience, as they were tossed back and forth with every sharp turn. Luckily the drive only lasted five minutes, coming to an end as the driver slammed on his brakes when they reached their destination.

Dickens still could see nothing as he was dragged out of the van, escorted down a hall, and guided to sit down in chairs.

He heard a voice say, "The Editor wants to see The Supervisor first," followed by a few soft footsteps, a door opening, and a door closing.

A guard removed the bag over Dickens' head. He was seated in a nice hallway outside an office door. The carpet was royal blue, which must have been brand new since the room stunk of new carpeting, and the décor was rather nice, albeit too gaudy for his taste. He wasn't entirely sure what he'd envisioned seeing when the bag was removed, an abandoned factory or something, but it certainly wasn't this.

The chair was comfortable, something he hadn't experienced since his Birth Life. He would have found it almost relaxing if it weren't for the armed guards, and if there wasn't shouting coming from inside the office. The door was closed but that didn't stop him from hearing every word as a man, apparently The Editor, yelled at The Supervisor.

"You know political correctness is not tolerated!" The Editor bellowed.

"I … I … I know, sir," The Supervisor said in a high-pitched voice. "But I didn't think it was …"

"I know you didn't think!" The Editor yelled, interrupting. "If you were thinking, I wouldn't have a Reviser turning his book into P.C. bull crap."

"Of course," The Supervisor said, "But I think the situation was …"

"The situation?" The Editor interrupted again. "I'll tell you the situation. The situation is I'd rather let these books go unrevised than to let them bend to the liberal agenda!"

Dickens watched as Guard 93 pressed his finger on his ear and began mumbling something to himself. Suddenly, a large-haired, overly makeup-ed woman came out of a nearby office holding a portable CD player. It looked futuristic to Dickens but was actually at least 25 years old. She lay the CD player on the floor next to The Editor's office. She hit a button on the top and a little door opened at a smooth pace. She placed a CD inside and hit 'play'.

"I understand," The Supervisor said, "But I …"

"Understand?" The Editor yelled, louder now than ever.

The woman pushed a few buttons on the device, turned a dial, and, a loud song boomed from within.

"Rejoice in the Lord always," the song bellowed.
And again I say rejoice.
Rejoice in the Lord always
And again I say rejoice."

It was clear this was intended to drown out the yelling, and it did make certain lines unintelligible, but it wasn't entirely effective.

"I don't know what I could have (UNINTELLIGIBLE)," The Supervisor said. "It's not like I (UNINTELLIGIBLE)"

"That's no excuse!!!" The Editor yelled. "The rules around here are (UNINTELLIGIBLE) if you don't understand (UNINTELLIGIBLE) for you."

"Rejoice! Rejoice!" the song bellowed.
Rejoice! Rejoice! Rejoice!
Rejoice! Rejoice!
Rejoice! Rejoice! Rejoice!"

"I do understand," The Supervisor said.

"You keep saying (UNINTELLIGIBLE)!!!" The Editor yelled. "But it's (UNINTELLIGIBLE) …"

The big-haired woman gave the guards a puzzled look and a shrug, and they returned the gestures with shrugs of their own.

The woman started singing along loudly, "This is the day, this is the day, that the lord hath made."

This made the yelling even more difficult to hear, but it still wasn't entirely drowned out.

"Why would I ever be (UNINTELLIGIBLE)," The Editor yelled. "When I (UNINTELLIGIBLE) writers back to life and (UNINTELLIGIBLE)!"

The woman began frantically gesturing toward the guards like a cocaine-snorting orchestra conductor, clearly wanting them to join her. They all looked at one another, and, reluctantly, began singing, too.

"Rejoice in the Lord always," the song screeched, both from the box and the makeshift choir.
And again I say rejoice.
Rejoice in the Lord always
And again I say rejoice.

This time it worked. All of the yelling was now unintelligible. As an added measure, the frantic woman clapped along, now slightly off beat.

It would have felt a lot like sitting outside a principal's office when you and a friend got in trouble — if it wouldn't have been for the gaggle of armed guards, and a batshit woman, singing church songs at the top of their lungs.

As the song came to an end, the music stopped for a moment, just in time for Dickens to hear The Editor yell, "Get the heck out of here, you heathen sack of snot!!!"

The Supervisor emerged from the office looking like half the man who had entered. The music suddenly started up again with a hymn Dickens recognized.

"What a friend we have in Jesus," the box screeched, as the woman tried to get the music to stop, and The Supervisor looked on in confusion.

"All our sins and griefs …" the music stopped abruptly, as the woman picked up the CD player, and hauled it back into the office from which she'd first appeared.

The Supervisor's look of confusion switched back to dejection, as he slowly walked away. But he stopped, turned back, and walked toward Dickens' chair. This made the guards uneasy, as they gripped their guns a little tighter.

Dickens could tell this was an emotional moment for The Supervisor, but he wasn't able to pinpoint which emotion. Anger? Sorrow? Compassion?

Finally, The Supervisor said in a pinched, squeaky voice, "I'm sorry I failed you, Mr. Dickens."

"I," he said, puzzled, "don't see how you failed me."

"Thank you," The Supervisor said, sincerely. "It was a pleasure working with such a distinguished …"

He was cut off, as two guards emerged from The Editor's office, threw a sack over The Supervisor's head, picked him up, and carried him off like a sack of flour. Guard 93 walked up to Dickens' chair.

"The Editor would like to speak to you now, Mr. Dickens," Guard 93 said.

He followed the guard into the office, and was told to have a seat across from a humongous desk. The man sitting at the desk, presumably The Editor, didn't look up at Dickens, his head was bowed in silent prayer. He didn't look like a man even capable of yelling in the manner he'd heard outside the office. He had curly hair, slightly on the long side. His build was thin, and had an exceptionally pointy face, which looked even pointier while bowed in prayer.

Dickens glanced around the office, which was decorated in a strange gold-plated theme. The walls were covered in pictures of The Editor posing with various people, none of whom Dickens recognized, but he surmised were important or famous.

The Editor slowly raised his head from his prayer, and looked directly at Dickens with eyes he felt were peeking into his very soul.

Suddenly the man formed an enormous, wide, toothy smile, and in a cheerful tone, almost as if laughing as he spoke, said, "Hello, Mr. Dickens. It's such an honor to meet you."

"Thank you. It's an honor …," Dickens trailed off. "Um … Mister …. what is your name, sir?"

The Editor didn't answer, but maintained his smile, which was way too big for the occasion, and continued that stare, his eyes never blinking. Dickens felt as if he should have been relieved he wasn't getting yelled at, but the smile, and the staring, were so creepy he might have preferred the yelling.

As the pause lingered, it was clear Dickens was on thin ice, but for reasons he didn't understand. The silence was his way of saying "I'm not telling you my name." It was both an answer to Dickens' question, and a threat.

"It's my understanding," The Editor said, continuing to speak through a smile, "in your Revision, you attempted to change the word 'cripple.'"

He enunciated harshly when saying the word "cripple"

"Yes, I did," Dickens said. "I'm afraid I don't understand. What have I done wrong?"

Ignoring the question, he said, "You saw the entry in the dictionary said 'cripple' is now an offensive term. Is that correct?"

"Yes, sir," Dickens said. "It wasn't offensive in my day."

"Of course, it wasn't," The Editor said. "You lived and died long before the liberals dispatched the P.C. police."

He nodded along, as if he understood.

"Thankfully, for your sake," The Editor said. "We've reviewed the security footage, and your story checks out."

"That's good news," Dickens said, still not fully grasping the situation.

"I know you weren't trying to be politically correct," he said, sounding as if those last two words made him want to vomit. "But if I catch wind of even a hint of political correctness, you'll be hobbling around like Tiny Tim."

Dickens was more frighten than ever, as the Editor continued to smile during, and after, he'd made a rather direct threat.

"There shouldn't be any more confusion," The Editor said. "All versions of THAT dictionary were removed from Revisers' desks and burned."

"But," Dickens said. "I've been asked to use modern American English. A dictionary is crucial to my Revising process.'

"I've already dispatched a team to find the least politically correct dictionary available," The Editor said. "When the team has completed this mission, we'll issue you a new dictionary."

Dickens nodded.

"Now that we've addressed that," The Editor said. "I want to tell you what a big fan I am of your work. Some of my most treasured childhood memories were watching "Christmas Carol" movies. The one with Mickey Mouse. The one with Bill Murray. I even like the one with the Muppets."

"Um, thank you, sir," he said, pleased to learn about the film adaptations of his book.

"You lived during a time when people loved Christmas," The Editor said. "When EVERYONE celebrated it, and EVERYONE was free to wish their fellow man a hearty, 'Merry Christmas.'"

Dickens reflected on how much controversy the book caused when it was published. Many religious people hated Christmas, and even viewed "A Christmas Carol" as a threat to Christianity. He kept these thoughts to himself.

"Mr. Dickens," he said. "I don't want to make you anxious, but in this despicable era, Christmas is under attack."

"Oh, no," Dickens said, as his internal anxiety was clearly manifesting in his voice, not from Christmas being attacked, but from the threat of violence.

"I can see your disappointment, and I am truly sorry," The Editor said, using words meant to convey empathy, but zero empathy came across. "We are at war. War against the atheists and the feminists and the reckless, lying media. They won't quit until Christmas is rendered obsolete, just like they did with Columbus Day."

Dickens nodded as if following along, but he was really making a mental list of questions to ask Nietzsche.

"Unfortunately, getting you here was the most difficult of all The Revisers," The Editor said. "There was a lot of red tape, but, after an intense covert operation, finally, you are here. This Revision is, by far, the most important."

"Why?" Dickens asked.

"Because when we reveal to the world we have uncovered the real "Christmas Carol," dismissing the old one as a fake," The Editor said, "we expose a vast conspiracy perpetrated by those who criticize Capitalism."

"All of that sounds great, sir," he said, "but …"

"These people seek to regulate Capitalism," The Editor said, still smiling. "Any regulation, leads to Communism, as I'm sure you know."

"I'm not sure I …" Dickens said.

"They hate Capitalism," he said, growing louder. "And they hate Christmas."

"So, how are the two …" he said, wondering why he continued to ask questions while The Editor was grandstanding.

"But once your Revision is unveiled," The Editor said, "They will have no choice but to admit their guilt for their failed attempts to alter the truth."

The irony of this was not lost on Dickens, but he knew sharing his true thoughts on the subject would help nothing.

"The entire world will shame them," he said, slowing down as he built toward his conclusion. "Even they will have to celebrate Capitalism. Even they will have to celebrate Christmas."

The Editor let silence hang for a moment, allowing Dickens to absorb the weight of his words.

"I'm sure they will," Dickens said, hoping he sounded sincere, though he wasn't. "But I can't help but wonder, if my book meant so much to you, why do you want it Revised?"

"Well, it wasn't your book," The Editor said. "It was the movies based on your book. I read the book for the first time a few years ago, and I have to say, even though I love how pro-Christmas it is, I'm not a fan of its anti-rich, pro-poor agenda."

Dickens had to suppress a chuckle, knowing that was the "agenda" of all his books.

"But where some people see an obstacle," The Editor said, "I see an opportunity. When we opened the Central Revision Complex, we were thinking too small. Having Nietzsche change 'God is Dead' to 'God isn't Dead,' or forcing Darwin to add passages to 'Origin of a Species' where he insists it was to be read 'Only For Entertainment Purposes'."

Dickens winced at this, understanding why Darwin refused to do the Revisions.

"That was small potatoes," The Editor said, his voice growing more passionate. "But with your Revision of A Christmas Carol, we have the opportunity to show the world the most treasured work of Christmas fiction ever written was hijacked and revised by Christmas-hating, poor-loving, bleeding-heart liberals! We must create the evidence to prove it was an extremist act of historical revision, and a cowardly act of guerilla warfare in the War on Christmas."

Despite the hypocrisy of this speech, he enjoyed hearing The Editor call his book "the most treasured work of Christmas fiction ever written." As soon as he noticed it, the enjoyment disappeared under a cloud of shame. He dismissed all feelings of flattery. For the sake of his sanity, he needed to prove he could overrule his ego. Realizing his convictions were still in charge, he eased into a state of mild contentment.

"We don't have much time," The Editor said. "Christmas is rapidly approaching, and you've got a lot of work to do."

The Editor pulled out a manuscript, and flipped through it, revealing it was peppered with small, square, yellow notes.

"I was looking over the pre-Revised draft," The Editor said, "and I have suggestions for how you can make the book less boring."

The suggestion of boredom erased Dickens' feelings of contentment.

"I understand how much criticism can hurt, Mr. Dickens," he said, "But I do a little writing myself, and have a better feel for modern language. Let me read to you one of my suggestions from the scene where you left off."

The Editor looked down at a larger-sized note affixed to the manuscript and read his suggested Revision:

"The Cratchit family proceeded to eat a meal they thought was wonderful, but was actually just poor and gross. They had fun, or should I say, they thought they had fun. Poor people act all noble and stuff, but it's really just disgusting to be poor. How do they expect us to think that's fun? Who do they think they are? But that's what you get when you are a freeloading loser, spending your entire life living off of the table scraps of a wealthy, job-creating saint."

He looked up from the manuscript, clearly impressed with his writing abilities. Dickens didn't have it within him to feign excitement, and he wasn't about to offer a compliment, even though it was clear The Editor was fishing for one.

"And after that," The Editor said, "Skip to the prayer and then just end the scene. You understand?"

Dickens nodded, unenthusiastically.

"Good," The Editor said. "I've filled the rest of the manuscript with notes. Some are just suggestions on how the text can be improved, since I really do respect the Reviser's autonomy, but other notes describe modifications I demand that you do. If you have any questions about whether a note is a suggestion or a demand, your new supervisor should be able to answer."

The Editor placed a binder clip on the manuscript and pitched it toward Dickens. It hit the desk with a loud slap.

"Have a blessed day," The Editor said, abruptly ending the meeting.

Dickens picked up the manuscript, as two guards grabbed his arms, and hoisted him out of the chair. They dragged him out of the office, and down a series of long corridors. Placing the bag over his head, they threw him into the back of the van, and sped off.

The guards escorted him back into the Revision Room more forcefully than usual. They pulled him up to his cubicle, and Guard 93 removed the bag from his head with a quick jerk. A man sat in Dickens' chair with his back turned and his boots kicked up on the desk. The guards released his arms but remained close.

The man at the desk spun around in his chair, revealing it was The Overseer.

No one spoke, as he sat, staring at Dickens in a manner similar to The Editor. But from him, there was no smile.

"Mr. Dickens," The Overseer said, breaking the uncomfortable silence. "I got a demotion because of you. I had four Revision Rooms under my authority."

He stood up, maintaining his menacing stare, and said, "Now I'm just in charge of one person. You!"

Nodding to the guards, he said, "Boys, you can stand down."

After the guards resumed their posts, he motioned for Dickens to sit down. The Overseer gripped the back of the chair, rolling it forward until the desk's edge poked into Dickens' stomach.

"I'm watching you," he whispered, leaning in so close his nose pushed against Dickens' cheek. "I'll watch you this close if I have to. Now, get back to work!"

While The Overseer continued to observe right next to his face, Dickens frantically scanned his computer screen for where he should resume the Revision. The Editor said to skip to the Cratchit's prayer, so he found the scene, highlighted the paragraphs before it, and hit delete. He grabbed the manuscript with The Editor's notes, looking for further direction.

"Very good," The Overseer said, finally moving his head back. "Do what we tell you to do, or I'll make YOU a cripple."

Dickens nodded. The Overseer walked away from the cubicle and took a seat where The Supervisor had sat.

He winced as he read every one of The Editor's notes. He'd written things like: "Make the beverage nonalcoholic" and "Make the Cratchits grateful for what Scrooge had given them."

It made him sick to even think about such changes, but he had no choice.

He began typing.

CHAPTER (Whatever): NAMELESS CHAPTER, BECAUSE NOTHING MATTERS

or

TRYING NOT TO FUCKING BARF WHILE WRITING

Bob Cratchit raised a glass of nonalcoholic punch to his family, and said, "A Merry Christmas to us all. God bless us!"

"God bless us!" bellowed the family.

In a sincere voice, Tiny Tim echoed, "God bless us, every one."

The entire family seemed sad. Clearly sad about Tiny Tim's suffering, but there was something else. Guilt. Shame. Humiliation. They knew Tiny Tim's suffering wasn't his fault.

The fault belonged to Bob.

Bob squandered the opportunities he'd had in life, choosing a life of poverty. If he'd chosen wealth, Tiny Tim could have seen a proper doctor, which would have ended his suffering.

"To Mr. Scrooge," Bob said, raising his nonalcoholic beverage, in hopes of stomping out the family's sadness. "Founder of the Feast."

"Founder of the Feast?" asked Mrs. Cratchit, her face red with anger. "I wish he were here. I'd give him a piece of my mind to feast upon."

"My dear," Bob said, mildly, "Mr. Scrooge deserves no blame. We are poor because of my bad decisions. And worse, I'm always looking for handouts."

Mrs. Cratchit lowered her head, starting to accept the truth.

"Mr. Scrooge is a self-made man," Bob said. "I should feel guilty for accepting such a high salary from such a man. Not to mention he is paying me to take off Christmas Day."

"He really did that for you?" Tiny Tim said.

"Indeed, he did, Tiny Tim," Bob said.

"I didn't realize that, Bob," Mrs. Cratchit said, remorseful. "He IS a generous man. I've been in denial. We deserve poverty."

"To Mr. Scrooge!" Tiny Tim said, raising his glass of milk.

"To Mr. Scrooge!" roared the rest of the family.

**

Dickens sat back from the screen. He wasn't feeling well, as if he might throw up. But The Overseer walked around the corner, suddenly.

"I don't hear typing, Mr. Dickens," he said.

Reluctantly, Dickens began typing.

**

Watching the Cratchit family realize the truth felt refreshing. I could have listened to them all day, but the Ghost had other plans.

We were instantly hovering outside the window of a lighthouse where we saw two weathered men, who could have been forlorn about having to work on Christmas. But they, sitting at a rickety table and sitting upon rickety chairs, joined hands, wishing one another a Merry Christmas. Again, without warning, we were on a ship at sea, where we floated through the entire ship. Every man, working or lounging, drunk or sober, was singing or humming a Christmas tune.

The Ghost was showing me that people under all sorts of circumstances can find a cheerful spirit at Christmas. I, a man of great wealth, was unable to find any. I needed to get my heart right and start celebrating Christmas. Before I could process this, we were back in the city, standing outside my nephew's house.

***

The steam whistle blew.

Dickens' guards escorted him out of the Revision Room, taking him straight to his room. Inside, his KFC bowl sat on the tray he used at breakfast. He even had cutlery and a napkin. Not having to eat with his hands should have made him happy, but he felt more isolated than ever, and more confused than ever, about what he'd done that was so wrong.

After eating, he folded the napkin neatly on the tray, which made him feel civilized, and homesick. He turned on the TV, causing the unfamiliar image of London to appear. He lay down on the bed and stared at the screen. If he had to be Resurrected, why did it have to be here? Why not back home?

He heard the rush of Revisers being ushered back to their rooms after dinner. Moments later, he heard tapping sounds coming from the bathroom.

Nietzsche: "what happened 2day?"

Dickens: "i don't know ... but i did something bad."

Nietzsche: "what?"

Dickens: "i tried 2 change the word cripple n my book ... dictionary said its offensive ... the supervisor got fired ... the editor threatened 2 break my legs."

Nietzsche: "u met the editor?"

Dickens: "yes"

Nietzsche: "u r the first reviser 2 meet him … the insider says knowing the editor's identity could end all this."

Dickens: "really?"

Nietzsche: "what's his name?"

Dickens: "i asked … but he didn't say"

Nietzsche: "can u describe him?"

Dickens: "skinny … pointy face … dark curly hair … never stopped smiling."

Nietzsche: "great … i need 2 tell the insider right now."

Dickens: "wait … do you know what i did wrong?"

Nietzsche: "no … i will ask the insider … gotta go."

Dickens: "wait!"

Nietzsche: "what? … i need 2 go!"

Dickens: "i don't know how long i can last here."

Nietzsche: "don't fight the suffering … embrace it!"

Dickens: "k"

Nietzsche: "just don't turn n 2 a drunk … like that awful hemingway."

Dickens: "who?"

Nietzsche: "u will meet him … need 2 go … have faith."

Dickens: "nietzsche is telling me 2 have faith?"

Nietzsche: "lol … have faith n intellect … we will outsmart them … they r not bright."

Dickens: "they have all the power."

Nietzsche: "they value faith … not knowing … that will be their downfall."

Dickens: "i hope u r right."

Nietzsche: "me too … gotta go!"

As he pushed himself off the bathroom floor, the small bottle of booze disguised as mouthwash, caught his eye. Without hesitation, he guzzled it down. He could follow Nietzsche's advice on most things, but, in his current state of mind, asking him to avoid drinking was advice he could not take.

The next morning, Dickens woke up early, eager to see what The Insider had written in his bible. Hopefully details about why he'd gotten in so much trouble when he changed the word "cripple," but more importantly, maybe there could be some details about plans to expose The Editor.

When the guards escorted him to his cubicle, he tried to look busy, even though he was in no mood for Revising. It would be too suspicious to grab the bible as soon as he walked in, so he pretended to look over the Editor's notes in the manuscript, and pretended to read over his most recent Revisions, until he could no longer wait.

He plucked the New Earth Bible from his shelf and flipped to Luke 17.

Nothing had changed from the day before. He flipped through the entire book of Luke, hoping messages were accidentally placed on the wrong page. He found nothing. He read over the previous scriptures in Song of Solomon, nothing new there either. He turned page by page through the entire bible. He still found nothing.

Dickens knew he should just let it be and wait until evening to see if Nietzsche knew what happened. But the feelings of excitement, eagerness, and disappointment were too much. He slowly scanned the room to see if any guards were looking at him. They weren't. In fact, the guards seemed distant, and no supervisors were around at all. This was rare, so he jumped at the opportunity.

He leaned in as close as he could to the cubicle wall between him and Nietzsche and whispered, "Hey! This is the same stuff from yesterday."

"That is disappointing," he said.

Nietzsche's voice sounded weird.

Dickens paused, before saying, "It IS disappointing."

"Oh," the voice whispered, "Did you think I was Mr. Nietzsche?"

Dickens screamed in his mind, "Nietzsche is gone! Nietzsche is gone! Nietzsche is gone!"

"I'm Niles Featherbottom," the man said. "I am a famous writer who you would never have heard of since you died before I became famous and wrote many novels that won many prestigious awards in my day."

What is he talking about? Where was Nietzsche? Was he caught? Did the CRC find out about The Resistance?

Dickens looked around the room again, and now the lack of attention from the guards, and the absence of supervisors, was very suspicious. It had to be a set up. Dickens' mind had been foggy since his Resurrection, but in his attempts to process this situation, his mind was slower than ever. The fogginess grew by the second.

What should I do? What do I say? What did I ask in the first place?

The man whispered, "Are you okay?"

"Well," Dickens mumbled, "I'm feeling a little light-headed."

This was true, and the only thing he could think of to say. This was a tricky situation. It required fast thinking he currently wasn't capable of executing.

"That is too bad," the man said. "But if you don't mind, I would very much like to discuss any thoughts you have about exposing these bastards."

Oh! He realized it when he heard the word "bastards." This person was faking a British accent, very badly.

"I suppose we could talk about that later, old bean," The Fake British Man said. "What were you disappointed about?

"Well," he said slowly, to buy more time. "I … well … just was asking if … well …"

In his mind, Dickens screamed, "Think! Think! Think!"

Looking down, he noticed the stack of notes from The Editor.

"The notes!" he said, a little too loudly. "For some reason I was expecting additional notes for my Revision. I can't remember why I thought that."

"Hmmm, quite," The Fake British Man said. "More notes would be jolly-good!"

"Sorry," Dickens said, "I can't think straight this morning, in addition to my lightheadedness."

"Oh, uh, cheers!" The Fake British Man said, awkwardly. "I do believe the esteemed Dr. Freud, you know, who also spent some time in our home jolly-good country, had some hypotheses for which he'd premised that lightheadedness had distinct cognitive influences on the brain's ability to think … well … you know … old bean … at its best cognitively, concerning knowledgeability and our ability to psychoanalyze with the ability to think straight."

"Of course!" Dickens said, assuming what he said about this 'Dr. Freud' was wrong. "I have not read that study, but you articulated it very well."

"Yes, quite," The Fake British Man said. "But it would be a shame to lose this opportunity, since the guards aren't watching. Are you aware of anyone planning an escape?"

"Well," he said, trying to sound sincere. "I'm not sure about that. I plan to obey our supervisors."

Too obvious. Dickens wanted to punch himself in the face.

"Oh, yes, yes," The Fake British Man said. "We should both be jolly-good fellows, and do our best. Perhaps another opportunity to discuss such conversations will present itself. Perhaps as early as this afternoon."

"Quite," he said, mimicking the fake British accent. "But I would find it even more jolly-good to hear more of your thoughts on psychology."

Dickens' berated himself with his inner dialogue, saying: Idiot! Idiot! Idiot! Why are you mimicking a fake British accent?

"Oh," The Fake British Man said. "We should try to do that."

"Good," Dickens said, in response to the confusing answer.

He waited for the man to say something else, but after a minute, he assumed the conversation had ended. He wasn't sure, though. He wasn't sure about anything. All he knew was they suspected something, were trying to bait him into incriminating himself with this ridiculous fraud of a Brit, and, most frighteningly, Nietzsche had disappeared.

Giving them the Revision they wanted was his only option. And, after that, hope for the best.

He looked over The Editor's notes. On the previous day, he'd left off when Scrooge and the Ghost arrived at his nephew's house. He began writing.

***

Inside, I saw my nephew, his wife, and loads of houseguests. The place, I'll admit, was tastefully furnished. So much better than Cratchit's gross, poor house. I mean, my nephew wasn't rich, but it appeared he did okay. I always assumed he was a freeloading loser, like Cratchit.

Yeah, I said it. Bob Cratchit is a loser. His meager earnings were his own fault, not mine.

Furthermore, if taxes weren't so high …

***

Dickens stopped, feeling as if he might get sick on his keyboard. He clinched his stomach, and took a couple of deep breaths to stabilize himself.

He noticed that the Revision Room, which was almost silent this morning, had grown noisier. The guards paid closer attention. The Overseer returned. This confirmed his suspicions that the Fake British Man had tried to set him up. It didn't work, and everything had returned to normal.

Very aware how closely he was being watched, he composed himself, and decided he needed to keep busy. He wrote, mixing in The Editor's bizarre prose to appease his captors.

***

My nephew's wife was talking trash about me. You know? The typical liberal bullshit, no doubt, regurgitated from the left-wing media.

My nephew came to my defense, saying, "Scrooge is a jolly-good man. He contributes much to society. He's mean because he isn't happy, but that's because he doesn't attend church."

"You're right," his wife said. "He just needs the joy of the Lord."

***

Dickens' nausea grew uncontrollable. He barely got his wastebasket under his mouth before throwing up. After several heaves of vomit, Custodian 8, who'd taken away his chair when he pissed himself, stood next to him. He swiftly replaced the wastebasket with another, handed him a wet rag to wipe his face, and had him rinse with mouthwash that tasted like minty kerosene.

When Custodian 8 had left, The Overseer was standing next to him.

"Okay," he said. "Start typing again."

Hopelessness spread through him like a drop of ink in a glass of water.

He wanted to return to his room, but there was no point in even asking. If he didn't continue the Revision, his suffering would grow even greater. He nodded to The Overseer, and reluctantly resumed typing.

***

"Uncle Scrooge said Christmas was a humbug," my nephew said. "He believed it too."

***

Dickens thought about how he'd replaced "Humbug" with "Go fuck yourself." He debated about whether to stick with the original, which The Editor would obviously prefer. Days earlier, he thought the change was hilarious. Now, he didn't care.

He decided to resume using "humbug," but didn't care enough to make the change earlier in the manuscript. He tried to move on to the next line but couldn't. A little of his previous fire still burned. Maybe no one else cared about inconsistency, but, even in a state of hopelessness, it still mattered to him.

Dickens deleted the previous line and Revised it.

***

"I wished Uncle Scrooge a Merry Christmas," my nephew said. "He told me to go fuck myself."

"He told you to go fuck yourself?" his wife asked. "Shame on him."

"He's a cantankerous old grouch," he said. "However, his offenses carry their own punishment, so he deserves no further punishment."

"I'm sure he is very rich, Fred," my nephew's wife said. "At least you have implied he's rich."

***

Dickens saw the nephew's original response was: "What of that, my dear? His wealth is of no use to him." Such a good line, he thought. Every ounce of his being screamed it was wrong to alter this line. He had to force himself to ignore that scream and continue typing.

***

"Yes," my nephew said. "He's wonderfully rich. It's a shame he doesn't spend more money on himself, though. And most importantly, he needs to get saved and begin celebrating Christmas."

"I have no patience for him," my nephew's wife added, and her sisters, also at the party, nodded in agreement.

"Well," my nephew said, "you are all stupid."

My nephew's wife and her sisters were shocked.

"Smart people, like my uncle, get rich." my nephew said. "If you don't value wealth, I have no patience for YOU."

My nephew's wife and her sisters all looked at one another, puzzled. After a moment, they began nodding to each other, coming to a silent agreement.

"You're right, my dear," my nephew's wife said. "I have been acting stupid."

Her sisters nodded along, having finally come to reason.

"Good," my nephew added, "I'm glad we settled that. Let's play some games."

***

Dickens slumped in his chair, as a part of him died.

***

My nephew and his party guests played a game of blind-man's bluff. One guy at the party, Topper, kept cheating so he could put his hands on one of the sisters. Objectively creepy, right? Wrong. Hopefully, people will find it creepy in the future, but not during this era. Nobody viewed Topper's inability to keep his hands to himself as inappropriate. It was playful, even cute.

They played another game called "Yes or No." The object of the game was for one person to think of something, and the others would guess what that thing was by only asking "yes" or "no" questions. My nephew went first. A brisk fire of questioning ensued, so fast it was impossible to keep track of who asked what.

Is it an animal? Yes
Is it a disagreeable animal? Yes
Is it a savage animal? Yes
Is it an animal that's found in the wild? No
Is it an animal found in London? Yes
Is it an animal sold in a market? No

With every question, my nephew roared with laughter.

Is it a dog? No
Is it a cow? No
Is it a horse? No
Is it a cat? No
Is it an ass?

With that last question, my nephew thought before answering, and then said, "Hmmm … Um … No!" laughing louder than before.

Then the sister, the one that creepy dude was tormenting, appeared to have an epiphany.

"I've got it!" the sister said.

"What is it?" my nephew asked, giggling.

"It's your Uncle Scrooge!" she yelled, with a fit of laughter.

The entire party burst into laughter, except my nephew.

"What?" my nephew yelled. "How dare you say such a thing?"

The sister walked away, cowering. The rest of the group went silent, stunned.

"The savage animal," my nephew spat out. "Was taxation on the wealthy."

"Ohhhhhh," they all said in unison.

"You see now?" my nephew said, before switching his attention back to the sister. "Scrooge has suffered enough. Instead of being villainized, he should be praised as a job-creator."

My nephew grabbed a glass of wine and raised it in the air.

"He's not always pleasant," my nephew said, as the guests grabbed their glasses. "But we would all be a bunch of jerks if we didn't raise a glass to his health. To Uncle Scrooge!"

They all raised their glasses, including the now ashamed sister, and took a drink.

The sister added, "And to even GREATER wealth!!"

She smiled at my nephew, which filled him with pride.

My nephew with tremendous enthusiasm, cried out, "To GREATER wealth!"

***

Dickens' nausea percolated again, a mix of shitty writing, and food too rich for his system. He grabbed the wastebasket and braced himself for a painful heave, but something in the wastebasket distracted him.

Sitting on top of the new plastic trash bag, poofed with air on the sides, sat, almost floated, a tiny piece of folded paper. Dickens hadn't touched the trash since Custodian 8 changed the bag. Someone else must have dropped it in. He forced another dry retch to justify stooping down near the wastebasket, palming the note as he sat up.

After taking some exaggerated deep breaths, he pretended to flip through The Editor's notes with his right hand, and smoothly unfolded the note with his left hand. He glanced down at the note, which said, "At 8:15 tonight, exit your room. Enter the room three doors down. Do it quickly."

Hope welled up within Dickens again, but it faded away just as quickly, as he considered it could be, yet another, set up.

He reread the note to check for clues it could be a set up. He flipped the note over, where more writing. clarified, "This is not a set up. Get rid of this note and keep typing."

He wadded up the note and, while pretending to yawn, covered his mouth with his left hand, and popped the note into his mouth. He lightly chewed it to break it down and swallowed it.

Of course, it still could be a set up, he thought. He didn't have a choice.

With mixed emotions, he went back to his writing.

***

The party guests raised their glasses, and cried out, "To GREATER wealth!"

I misjudged my nephew. He told his guests they would have been jerks not to drink to my health — and he was right. But perhaps I too had been a bit of a jerk to him. Maybe "jerk" is too strong, since I WAS right about everything I said. But, you get the point.

The Ghost signaled it was time to leave. When outside, I saw he had grown much older since we'd first met. His hair and beard were gray. His face a Caucasian prune.

"My life is brief," the Ghost said. "It ends at midnight. In just a few minutes."

I nodded as if I understood, but something distracted me.

"What is that protruding from your robe?" I asked. "Is it a foot or a claw?"

"It's a claw, or something equally icky," the Ghost replied, lifting up his robe. "Look here."

From underneath his robe, the heads of two children popped out; vile, dreadful, and hideous children. They knelt down at his feet, leeching to his robe.

"Look at it!" the Ghost said, screeching with the urgency of a person showing their doctor an angry genital rash.

It was a boy and a girl. Dirty, scowling, wolfish. No perversion of humanity has produced monsters as repulsive as these two children.

I attempted to say one of those obligatory phrases like "they are adorable" or "they look just like you," but I couldn't force out the words.

"Are they yours?" I asked, the best I could do.

"They are the offspring of mankind," the Ghost said, looking down at them with pity.

***

Dickens stopped his writing and looked over at the notes The Editor had written about this scene — the longest note he'd written about the text.

"I like this part, although I think you might want to change where the children are located within the robe. Maybe they are riding on his shoulders. The clergy have a bad reputation, which is entirely the Catholics' fault, and I don't want to feed into that. Anyway, I like the idea of monster children being Mankind's children."

Dickens stopped reading the note and read ahead to remind him what had been written in the original manuscript. "This boy is Ignorance. This girl is Want. Beware them both, but most of all, beware this boy."

He returned to reading The Editor's notes.

"Instead of 'Ignorance' and 'Want,' we should make them 'Poverty' and 'Whining'. Or maybe even add a third child called 'Political Correctness.'"

Dickens read that note, and it repulsed him, even though he was still confused about this whole "Political Correctness" thing. He loved this scene in the original. Scrooge asked if the children had no refuge and the Ghost fired back at Scrooge with his own words, saying "Are there no prisons? Are there no workhouses?"

He decided to cut out the scene about the children. If The Editor didn't like it, Dickens would throw his words back at him, (Ghost of Christmas Present-style) saying the modern reader would think keeping children under your robe was deviant behavior no matter where the children are located underneath the robe. Dickens had no idea if that was the way modern readers would perceive the scene, but The Editor had given him a reason to ax the scene, so he did.

Returning back to Scrooge:

**

The bell struck twelve.

I looked around for the Ghost, but he had vanished into the darkness. Before I could worry about his whereabouts, a Phantom floated toward me, like a mist along the ground.

**

The steam whistle sounded, indicating the end of the work day. Dickens was filled with strong fear and excitement about what awaited him at 8:15.

After dinner with the other Revisers, and still no sign of Nietzsche, Dickens returned to his room where he, once again, was alone with his thoughts. He replayed the day's events in his mind, attempting to find clues about what had happened, and what he might encounter at this mysterious meeting at 8:15. Ideally, he'd have a face-to-face meeting with The Insider, but it never left his mind that it could be an ambush.

Not only did he not know who'd left the note in his trash, but he realized now how much he'd accepted as true without concrete evidence. He'd believed that the person tapping messages was Nietzsche. He'd believed that the messages in his bible were left by The Insider. He assumed the British man was an imposter, but how did he even know the man with the German accent was really Nietzsche?

Of all the thoughts rolling around in his mind like a cement mixer, the one that kept popping up the most, as he stared at the digital clock on his nightstand, was: "Why does modern man feel the need to have clocks with large, glowing numbers?" In his Birth Life, he never considered it a hassle to look at clock hands. To him, digital clocks seemed like a superfluous invention, but, even though it bothered him, it was a welcome distraction from his more troubling thoughts.

When the clock flipped from 8:14 to 8:15, his room went dark, followed by a nerve-rattling alarm. A guard's voice started coming from the speakers in his room, but the alarm almost entirely drowned it out. Dicken didn't hesitate. He ran to the door, opened it, and ran out.

The hallway was dark except for one red light flashing to the rhythm of the alarm, which was much louder in the hall. He started jogging down the hall to the right of his room, but he saw the third door from his room was closed. He twisted the doorknob. It was locked.

Taking a deep breath, he attempted to figure out if he'd made a mistake. He was positive that the note said, "three doors down," and thought it had said to head right, but now he wasn't sure. Too bad he'd eaten the note. His memory was so bad right now it couldn't be trusted. He decided to check the third door in the other direction.

He got a few steps in the other direction when he heard a voice say, "Hey! Dickens!" He turned his head and ran back to the other door, which was now ajar, but, as he got close to the door, it flew open for him to run inside. The door slammed behind him.

Dickens bent down, holding himself up with his hands on his knees as he took deep breaths. His heart pounded, from the excitement, but it also was the first time he'd run since his Birth Life. The man who let him in stood in a half-squat stance, bracing himself to open the door.

"Hi," Dickens said. "I guess you know me, but …"

"I'm Will," the man said curtly, motioning for Dickens to move farther into the room.

Will had a British accent. A real British accent. The first British accent he'd heard since his Birth Life. Suddenly he felt less alone.

Four candles placed against each wall illuminated Will's room, giving it a warm and inviting feel. It looked like a mirror image of his room, but with different photographs on the walls. Skimming the bookshelf, he was amused to see a series of hardback books labeled "Complete Works of Charles Dickens."

He reached out to remove one of the books from the shelf when someone knocked on the door, tapping the letters "K" and "M" in the code Nietzsche taught him. Will threw the door open, which caused the alarm coming from the hall to blare much louder, but as another man ran in, he closed the door behind him, muffling the alarm sound. The man who'd just run in, paused for a moment to catch his breath, but then took a long look at Dickens.

Turning back to Will, the man asked, "Is that him?"

"Yeah," Will said with a loud whisper. "It's him. Dickens."

The other man walked up and extended his hand for a shake, gripping Dickens' hand firmly.

"It is very good to see you, sir," the handshaker said, continuing the overly enthusiastic handshake.

"It's good to see you, too," Dickens said, wincing. "But may I have my hand back?"

"I'm so sorry," the man said, blushing as he let go. "I'm a little excited."

Someone knocked on the door, tapping the letters "M" and "T." The door flew open once again, and another man ran in furiously, the door slamming behind him. The handshaker gave this man a quick wave, and then returned his attention to Dickens.

"We've met before," the handshaker said to Dickens. "At a party in London. We only talked for a minute."

"I don't remember you, but I'm willing to bet your head wasn't shaved," Dickens said. "And I'm afraid I can't place your accent."

"Of course, you can't," the handshaker said, grinning. "I was born in Prussia and then lived in Paris, Belgium, and finally ended up living in London, while in exile."

Another knock, tapping out "E" and "H," caused Will to whip the door open. A heavyset man ran in. The handshaker gave him a quick nod of recognition, and turned back to Dickens.

"I had enormous hair and an enormous beard," the handshaker said. "The chance of you remembering me was slim. I was a nobody during my Birth Life."

"And your name?" Dickens asked.

"I'm Karl," the handshaker said. "Marx. I must say, I found your work inspirational. You deeply cared about the common man, and weren't afraid …"

"Hey!" the heavyset man said to Dickens, with a loud American accent. "Don't believe anything you hear from that commie bastard."

The man walked up to Karl, swaggering as if preparing to fight, and put Karl in a headlock, playfully patting his bald head.

While he winced from the man holding his head, Karl said, "This is Hemingway."

Hemingway laughed loudly, let go of Karl's head, and walked toward Dickens.

"So, you're the great Charles Dickens?" Hemingway asked.

"I'm not sure about great," Dickens said, playfully. "But, yes, I'm Charles Dickens."

Hemingway gave Dickens a good-humored punch on the shoulder, and said, "Hell, it's great to meet you."

The punch didn't seem intended to hurt, but it still did.

Through clinched teeth, Dickens said, "It's nice to meet you too."

"Of course, it is," Hemingway said.

He gave Dickens a firm punch on his other shoulder and walked off. A rush of memories of encounters with arrogant Americans from his Birth Life flashed through his head.

"Hemingway is a great guy," Karl said to Dickens. "But, Christ, that man annoys me."

Dickens laughed, rubbing the sore spot on his shoulder from Hemingway's punch.

They gathered in a circle near Will's bed, as the man who ran in between Karl and Hemingway began to address the group.

"Gentlemen," the man said, in an American accent, "Hugo and the others won't be with us tonight. The door to the French and Spanish wing closed when I tripped the alarm. We'll have to do this on our own."

Dickens noticed that his eyes were beginning to adjust to the dim lighting, as he watched the American open up a messenger bag slung over his arm and remove a notebook.

"We only have five minutes," the man said, raising his voice loud enough to be heard over the alarm. "If we haven't met, I am Mark Twain. I would love to get to know each of you, but there's no time."

They all nodded.

"Okay," Twain said. "The Resistance was compromised. It appears our lines of communication were intercepted. Also, Nietzsche has disappeared."

The men gasped.

"Have you seen anything unusual?" Twain asked the group.

Dickens waited for the others to speak, but when no one did, he said, "The man who replaced Nietzsche has a fake British accent."

"We've seen that before," Twain said. "It's always the same guy. Probably some failed actor."

"You should have heard his 'Prussian accent,'" Karl said, with finger quotes. "It was so ...."

"To get us back on track," Twain said, interrupting. "The Insider has instructed us to shut everything down immediately. And I'm sorry to say that also means no more booze."

The men groaned.

Twain reached into his messenger bag and scooped out a bundle of tiny vodka bottles, dumping them on the bed.

"This is the last of the stash from the custodian's closet," Twain said. "Try to make it last."

The men jumped on the bottles like a pack of wolves. In the fury, Dickens only grabbed four, which he quickly slipped into his pockets. The overly aggressive Hemingway got the most, which disappointed everyone.

"Now," Twain said. "I need you all to get the books together and place them in my bag. I expect they'll flip these rooms very soon. Getting caught with contraband is one thing. Getting caught with the books is different."

Will selected four thick books from his bookshelf and passed them to Karl, who tossed them on the bed.

"I don't know what the CRC learned or how they learned it," Twain said. "Or if we'll ever be able to meet like this again."

Twain looked at his watch, which Dickens was pleased to see wasn't digital, and said, "You've got three minutes."

"It's a waste of time," Hemingway said. "We need to do what I've been saying the whole time and …"

"Your thoughts have been roundly rejected," Will said. "You imbecile!"

"You call me that one more time, Shakes-queer," Hemingway yelled, "and I'll …"

Dickens tuned out Will and Hemingway's arguing, as he felt a wave of excitement rush over him. "Will," whose bedroom he was standing in right now, was William Shakespeare. He badly wanted to gush about what a big fan he was, but shook the thought, knowing Twain was right about the lack of time.

"I'll stab you in the thorax," Shakespeare said.

"I'll throw your tinkerbell ass across this …" Hemingway said.

"Stop it!" Twain yelled, interrupting the arguing. "You are wasting precious time."

Dickens said, "What are in these books?"

Karl reached over, grabbed one and handed it to Dickens.

"This one is fun," Karl said, "But it does us no good right now."

Dickens opened it up and flipped through a few pages. It was a copy of War and Peace, but with pages replaced with color photographs of naked women, and men.

Karl handed him another book, as Dickens reluctantly closed the "fun" one and tossed it back on the bed. Hemingway picked it up and began flipping through it, as Shakespeare looked over his shoulder.

"That one is filled with possible escape routes, maps of the building and all of that." Karl said.

"Yes," Twain said. "Look at that one carefully. If you ever find yourself in any of the vulnerable areas of the building, make a run for it and head for one of these places."

He pointed on a map to a couple of newspaper and TV station locations. Dickens also saw where "police station" was labeled with, "Do not go here."

Karl held up the third book, and said, "And this one is a scrapbook of all the newspaper and magazine clippings we've discovered or smuggled in."

Dickens looked up from the map as Karl flipped through the book of newspaper scrapping.

"But, as you can see," Karl said. "These aren't helpful for any plans of escape. They help us understand the outside world. It gives us some insights into …"

"Wait!" Dickens yelled, as he saw a picture Karl had flipped past.

Dickens tossed the book of maps on the bed and grabbed the newspaper scrapbook. He flipped back a few pages and angled the book toward a candle. Sure enough, he had seen it correctly. He turned the book around, held it up for the other men, and pointed at a photograph in a newspaper clipping. The headline for the article stated: "Megachurch pastor says he's forgiven disgraced journalist."

"That's him!" Dickens said.

"Who?" Shakespeare asked.

"The Editor," Dickens said.

Twain grabbed the book and looked at it in amazement. The others rushed around to see the photograph as well.

"How do you know that?" Hemingway asked.

"I met with him yesterday," Dickens said. "Nietzsche said he was going to tell The Insider."

"I guess they caught him before he had the chance," Karl said.

Hemingway said, "Uh, no shit, you commie pile of …"

"You met with him here?" Twain asked, interrupting. "Somewhere in the Central Revision Complex?"

"No," Dickens said. "They took me someplace else. In an automobile. To the Editor's office."

"Oh, Dickens," Twain said, excited. "You have no idea how big this is."

"Really?" Dickens asked.

"Yes," Twain said. "This man is no editor. That's Kenneth Rich. The most famous TV preacher in the United States. He pastors a church with 90,000 members. It's just a few minutes away from the CRC."

"Why on earth," Shakespeare said, "would a clergy behave this way?"

"I'm not sure," Twain said. "But he's a man who lures in all of these people, saying God wants to make them rich. Even worse, he never condemns anything. Horrendous things. Atrocities. He has seriously failed to condemn the behavior of Nazis, saying only that God loves them."

"So, the church is misdirection while he Revises history?" Karl asked.

"It could be," Twain said. "I'm guessing he uses the money he rakes in from the church to fund the Central Revision Complex. I always assumed it was a government operation, but maybe not."

Hemingway grabbed the scrapbook away from Twain, looked at it closely, and said, "Wait! Is this one of mine?"

"What?" Twain asked, taking the book back from Hemingway.

"It is," Hemingway said, tapping on the article with his finger. "I wrote this."

"They have you write news articles in addition to your Revising?" Dickens asked.

"All they've ever asked me to do is write fiction stories," Hemingway said. "It's some of my best work."

"Fiction stories about what?" Twain asked.

"About widespread corruption," Hemingway said, pointing to the newspaper. "That one is about a journalist. A muckraker who takes down corrupt people. It turns out he's really a spy for a foreign government. The victim in my version wasn't a pastor. He was a four-star general. He takes the high road. He refused to condemn the journalist who tried to take him down."

"How did your fiction stories wind up in a newspaper?" Shakespeare asked.

"Yeah," Karl said. "How did this happen?"

"Oh, come on!" Hemingway growled, rolling his eyes. "They are using what I thought was fiction as propaganda."

"That's not just propaganda," Twain said. "That's creating conspiracy theories."

"How did this work?" Dickens asked. "The Supervisor would come up and ask you to write a fiction story about corruption?"

"Not exactly," Hemingway said. "It always came straight from The Overseer. He would give me a jumping off point, and I'd run with it. With this one he said he had an idea for a story about a journalist who claimed to be uncovering corruption, but wound up being more corrupt than anyone else."

"How do we know you're not in on it, too?" Karl asked.

"Uh," Hemingway said. "If I were in on it, why would I tell you?"

"Uh," Karl said. "How do we even know you're the real Ernest Hemingway?"

"How do I even know there WAS a writer named Ernest Hemingway?" Shakespeare asked.

"Hmmm," Hemingway said. "Hang on. This is a great novel idea. Let me take some notes."

Karl and Shakespeare exchanged a glance, before Shakespeare said, "Okay. You're definitely a writer, but still, how do we …"

"Enough!" Twain yelled. "In the last few minutes, we have discovered more about this place than we have in the last few years. All of the revelations, especially The Editor's identity, are more than we need to blow the lid off this thing. But it's not over. So be careful."

They all nodded.

Twain looked down at his watch, and said, "Time's up! Get back to your rooms."

He started putting the books into his book bag, zipped it up, and slung it over his shoulder.

"Gentlemen," Twain said. "It's been great working with you. Hopefully I'll see you all again, very soon. But if not, please don't let this place pollute your impression of Americans. We are not all bad. Most of us are very good."

"This place hasn't polluted my impression of Americans," Shakespeare said. "Hemingway has."

They all had a hearty laugh — Hemingway laughing the loudest — and rushed to the door. Twain opened it up, looked both ways, and motioned for all of them to follow. They all ran out into the hall and into their rooms.

When Dickens had closed his door behind him, he slumped down in his chair.

He was amazed at what he had just witnessed. Some of the greatest writers of all time, including fucking Shakespeare, were meeting together, plotting an escape. And he, Charles Dickens, had secured the key piece of information. He was proud and, for a moment, somewhat grateful he had been Resurrected.

He felt an almost overwhelming need to celebrate, and then remembered he had four bottles of vodka in his pockets. He walked into the bathroom, quickly unscrewed one, and chugged it. Mindlessly, he unscrewed another and gulped it down. Minutes later, he'd drank all four.

Abruptly, the alarm stopped blaring, and the lights flashed back on. He'd grow accustomed to the darkness, and the lights now hurt his eyes. He stumbled out of the bathroom, turned off the lights, and plopped onto his bed.

Getting in bed, while buzzing on alcohol, had become a familiar feeling, but getting in bed completely drunk was new. He thought about how much Nietzsche would have disapproved of this behavior, but he didn't feel bad. But he did hope he would be able to see his friend soon.

Drunkenly, he laughed out loud, though, of something Nietzsche had said during one of his rants about alcohol, when he mentioned that "horrible Hemingway." He didn't know what the man did in his Birth Life, but "horrible Hemingway" did seem like an apt description.

He laughed again, slipping into a very pleasant sleep.

The following morning, Dickens awoke in great spirits, and, surprisingly, without a trace of a hangover. He devoured his daily English muffin and replayed last night's events in his mind. When the guards arrived at his room, he cheerfully walked along, feeling optimistic his suffering would soon end.

But when Dickens was led into the Revision Room, he felt a palpable, unnerving vibe. Something had gone wrong.

The Overseer was sitting at Dickens' desk, in his chair, flipping through the New Earth Bible, the one in which he'd received messages. There were four armed guards standing around his cubicle, in addition to the usual one escorting him from his room. All eyes turned to him.

Without looking up, The Overseer said, "Good morning, Mr. Dickens."

"Good morning," Dickens said, with worry and confusion.

"I decided to come in early and do a little light reading," The Overseer said, as he lifted up the New Earth Bible.

Dickens swallowed, and said, "It's a good book."

"THE good book," The Overseer said forcefully. "But it looks like your copy wasn't inspired by God."

Dickens tried to think of excuses that wouldn't compromise anyone else, but his brain was foggier than ever.

"How did you get wrangled into plotting a coup?" The Overseer asked. "You've hardly been here a week."

"I don't follow, sir," Dickens said, trying to sound innocent. "Mr. Nietzsche and I were just having a little fun adding extra text in that bible."

"Ugh," The Overseer said. "You must really think I'm stupid."

Dickens knew better than to respond to this.

"I bet you don't even think Americans know how to read, do you?"

"Of course, you know how to read," Dickens said.

"Your friend tried to escape," The Overseer said. "The police caught him and immediately returned him to us."

Dickens lowered his head. The plans really were foiled.

"We anticipated someday a Reviser would make a break," The Overseer said. "This is why the Central Revision Complex was built underneath an insane asylum for particularly dangerous criminals. That CRC on the back of your jumper bears the same initials of the Criminal Rehabilitation Center. Escapees will obviously be thought of as insane, dangerous criminals. Especially those claiming to be a famous, historical figure."

Dickens nodded along. Building the place underneath an asylum was pretty clever. He was impressed. These people had proven themselves to be unbelievably dense on one hand, but surprisingly clever at times, too. Is it possible they pretended to be stupid?

"We started sniffing around," The Overseer said. "And found disturbing things written in a whole bunch of bibles."

Dickens knew there was no point in denying, but there was too much to process, including the question of what Nietzsche was planning to do when he escaped. Was he trying to make use of the information he'd gained from Dickens' description of The Editor? Maybe he had a plan for getting help? Was he acting in his own selfish interests?

"Did you really think we wouldn't find out?" The Overseer asked.

Dickens' heart sank. He knew he ought to play dumb until he had a better plan. But he couldn't. All of a sudden, the situation seemed too ridiculous to be real, and he decided to respond to The Overseer's question as if there would be no consequences for telling the truth.

"Yes," Dickens said, chuckling to himself. "I assumed you wouldn't find out."

"Is that so?" The Overseer yelled, his face growing red with anger.

"Yes," Dickens said. "You people are, by far, the stupidest mammals I've ever met."

The Overseer stood up and punched him in the stomach. Dickens doubled over in pain.

"I don't see you laughing now," The Overseer yelled. "We beat you bastards when we founded this country. And we beat your asses … uh … a bunch of times since then. I'm not going to sit around here while you …"

Before The Overseer could finish his rant, Dickens quickly worked himself up onto all fours, stumbled to a standing position, and ran toward the main exit.

"Stop him!" The Overseer yelled.

A barrage of gunfire erupted. It felt like hundreds of bullets penetrated his back, like being tenderized with exploding hammers.

He collapsed in unbelievable pain, as the shooting stopped. Dickens lay still for a moment, but then continued to crawl toward the exit, as another force of bullets rained over him. He felt wet as the blood spilled from his body.

The pain subsided. Everything faded to black.

Dickens woke up feeling sick, tired, and mentally limp, like a hangover with an acute case of déjà vu. He thought to himself, "Where am I? I thought I was dead?" which came with another wave of déjà vu. The smells of the room suddenly came to his conscious mind, and he knew where he was.

He, literally, with no sense of irony, wished he were dead.

Someone began shaking his arm, and he opened his eyes. He was in the Resurrection Room, and The Doctor stood over him.

"Dickens," The Doctor said, authoritatively, now standing at the foot of the bed. "Rise and come forth!"

Dickens tried moving his arms, but this movement was yanked to a halt with a loud clank of chains. He tried to move his legs, which were also restrained.

"I love doing that to people freshly Resurrected," The Doctor said, chuckling. "Get it? It's what Jesus said when he raised Lazarus from the dead."

Dickens understood it, but it wasn't worth acknowledging. Not for The Doctor. Especially not now.

"Did you really think you could escape?" The Doctor asked. "You seemed so smart."

"I had to try," Dickens groaned out.

"Did you?" The Doctor asked, condescendingly. "All you managed to do was create more work for me."

"Yeah," he said, snorting. "That alone makes it worthwhile."

The Doctor backhanded Dickens across the face. He flinched, which was excruciating, as the chains made any movement painful.

The door to the Resurrection Room flew open, startling both Dickens and The Doctor. Numerous armed guards charged into the room, followed by The Editor, with his thin, pointy face and plastic smile. The Doctor lowered his head and staggered out of the way, like a beta dog submitting to its alpha.

As The Editor approached Dickens, he began a slow, sarcastic clap.

"Nicely done," The Editor said, mocking. "You just made your life far more difficult."

"This isn't MY life!" Dickens yelled. "I spent MY life offering a voice to the poor, and I'm not going to help you turn heroes into villains."

"You have no choice," The Editor said, bluntly.

"You're the one without a choice," Dickens yelled. "Kill me as many times as you want. I am not Revising another word."

"I suppose you are right," The Editor said. "You're a stubborn man."

The Editor nodded toward a guard, who nodded back, turned, and marched down the hall.

"Charles," he said, slowly walking toward Dickens. "There's no shame in admitting ignorance. Modern man isn't smarter than those in your era, but we do know what's best for the world."

Dickens wanted to spit in The Editor's face, but his mouth was too dry.

"The world is filled with poor people," The Editor continued, with a faint smile. "God chose to make them poor. What your work did was create feelings of empathy for people who didn't deserve it. God was trying to teach them a lesson. Your books taught them to blame others."

"You are deranged!" Dickens yelled.

"Mr. Dickens," The Editor said, smiling wider than ever. "During your time, the streets were piled in horse dung, since horses were your finest mode of transportation. You never had a chance to talk on a telephone or even see an electric light bulb. Our ways might confuse you, but you need to accept we know what's best."

Another four guards, along with The Overseer, rushed into the room, dragging along Nietzsche, who was bound in chains. His face was swollen and bruised. He had dark circles under his eyes/ Perhaps from a beating. Perhaps from sleep deprivation. Perhaps from both.

"Mr. Dickens said we were a bunch of dumb mammals," The Overseer said to The Editor, as he gave Nietzsche a light slap on the face. "Mr. Nietzsche must have thought the same thing, but it looks like he got outsmarted by a bunch of dumb mammals."

"That's right, Charles," The Editor said, pointing to Nietzsche. "This is exactly my point. Friedrich is smart and look where it got him. We are so much more advanced, you should think of us as God. You can't understand our ways. You shouldn't even try."

"I managed to figure out who you are, Kenneth Rich" Dickens said. "And all you're doing is repackaging the horseshit that reckless capitalists peddled back in 1843."

The Editor seemed impress.

"I didn't know that happened in your day," The Editor said. "That's a very valuable insight. Now I can look it up, see where they went wrong, and make sure I don't make the same mistakes."

"It wasn't their tactics that failed," Dickens said. "It was their message. Maybe you should try learning from history instead of changing it."

"Oh, Mr. Dickens," The Editor said, condescendingly. "It's true that if you don't know your history you are doomed to repeat it. Which is why we need to erase the bad ideas from history, and replace them with good ideas. If the bad ideas from the past never existed, we can't repeat them."

"That makes no sense," Dickens said. "Also, I thought God frowned upon lying."

"God works in mysterious ways," The Editor said, pointing toward the Resurrection Machine. "Take this machine, for example. God can even use an atheist scientist. Dr. Alex Wilderman invented the Machine and then God blessed us with the means to acquire it. Alex even showed us how to use it, before passing away. Don't you see? This is a perfect example of God using an evil vessel to accomplish his will."

The Editor paused, seemingly for dramatic effect, like he was in a stage play.

"Mr. Dickens and Mr. Nietzsche," The Editor said. "The two of you, despite your wayward paths, are getting the chance to accomplish God's will."

"God's will?" Dickens said. "This is about your will. You are the one who wants to change history."

The Overseer blurted out, "It's clearly God's will that we change history."

The Editor held up his hand toward The Overseer in a "Calm Down" fashion, and said, "I think both of you are failing to see how you could benefit. Especially you Mr. Nietzsche."

The Editor signaled to The Overseer, who was carrying a backpack, and said, "I have a photograph I'd like you to see."

The Overseer removed an accordion folder, pulled out a stack of papers, and handed it to The Editor.

The Editor sifted through the files as he said, "You both will find this very interesting."

He removed an 8X10 photograph and held it up to Nietzsche's face. He walked it over, so Dickens could see it too, and then held it back in front of Nietzsche's face.

Pointing at the old lady in the photograph, The Editor asked, "Do you know this woman?"

Nietzsche turned his head away, so he couldn't see it. The Editor motioned to the guards who grabbed Nietzsche's head, and twisted his neck around, so he couldn't look away.

"She's much older, but you still know who this is, don't you?" The Editor asked.

Nietzsche still refused to answer.

The Editor nodded toward The Overseer, who sat his backpack down and swiftly punched Nietzsche in the stomach. He doubled over in pain, coughing.

"You know who this woman is," The Editor said, leaning down with his ear in Nietzsche's face. "And I want to hear you say it."

Nietzsche took a deep breath and mumbled something unintelligible into The Editor's ear.

"Repeat that, Mr. Nietzsche," The Editor said, looking back toward Dickens. "Say it so everyone can hear."

After more coughs, and another deep breath, Nietzsche quietly said, "My sister."

"Your little sis, Elizabeth," The Editor said, maintaining his enormous grin. "Was that so hard?"

Nietzsche let out another loud coughing fit, as The Editor walked over to Dickens and held the photograph up close to his face.

"Lizzy is handing this man a walking stick that once belonged to your God-hating friend," The Editor said, pointing to the man opposite of Elizabeth in the photograph. "Any idea who this man is?"

Dickens took a long look and shook his head.

"I didn't expect you to," The Editor said, his voice taking on a preacher's cadence. "But he's a man that every man, woman, boy, and girl alive today can identify."

He walked the photograph over to a few of the guards and said, "Gentlemen, nod if you know the name of the man shown in this photograph?"

They all nodded.

"You!" The Editor said, pointed in the direction of Guard 93. "Please identify this man for Mr. Dickens."

"It's Adolph Hitler, sir," Guard 93 said, with a booming voice.

"You!" The Editor said, pointing to Guard 84. "Tell Mr. Dickens why this man is so famous."

"Yes, sir," Guard 84 belted, as if answering a drill sergeant. "He was a German dictator, sir! Responsible for the death of millions of Jews, sir!"

"Six million," The Editor said, turning back to Nietzsche. "Did you know about this?"

Nietzsche nodded, dejected.

"She took care of you, sort of, when you went insane," The Editor said, to Nietzsche. "But when you died, Lizzy found a notebook you never intended to publish, and twisted your words into an anti-Semitic manifesto. That book was used to validate the Nazi movement, and your name will forever be linked to one of the darkest times in world history."

Silence hung in the room as The Editor slowly walked up to Nietzsche.

"You know," The Editor said. "A lot of people don't get along with their siblings, but you, Mr. Nietzsche, might have had the all-time worst sibling. It's not like Cain killed six million Abels."

More silence. Dickens could now see why he was such an influential preacher. He slow-walked the room through all of his points, using the false interaction of asking questions of which everyone already knew the answer, just so he could make a grand point about the answer being correct. But the silence. His use of silence was spectacular. He knew how to hold the silence right before a great line. It built anticipation, and made the lines, the ones he wanted to stand out the most, hang in the air, until the precise moment he was ready to pull the trigger.

"You lived your life like an atheist monk, Mr. Nietzsche" The Editor said. "But well before we even got a chance to intervene, your sister made sure you'd never be remembered that way."

He held onto a long silence, and then pulled another trigger.

"Mr. Nietzsche," The Editor said. "Your history has already been changed."

Turning to Dickens, The Editor said, "Charles, wouldn't you say that's horrible?

"Of course," Dickens eked out.

The Editor turned to The Overseer and asked, "Young man, if you had something evil tainting your legacy, wouldn't you want it erased from history?"

"No doubt," The Overseer said, enthusiastically. "I wouldn't think twice."

"'Wouldn't think twice' is the correct answer," The Editor said. "Mr. Nietzsche, I'm offering you the opportunity to Revise your legacy, in exchange for Revisions to your books."

Turning to Dickens, The Editor said, "Charles, I'll extend the same offer to you."

A look of horror formed on Dickens' face.

"Your legacy is fine," The Editor said. "In fact, historically, there aren't many authors more respected."

Dickens' look turned to confusion.

"But a legacy can always be changed," The Editor said. "Historians are always uncovering unflattering facts."

The Editor pulled out another paper from the stack and held it up to Dickens' face. It was a photocopied page from Oliver Twist, with a smattering of words highlighted.

"Take a good look, Charles," The Editor said. "We didn't doctor this."

The Editor walked over to the guards again, held it up for them to see, and said, "One of Charles' most famous characters is a man named Fagin, who's an old greedy thief. But throughout Oliver Twist, Charles frequently chose not to call the character 'Fagin.' Rather, he chose to use the term I've highlighted on this page."

Dickens felt sick to his stomach now, realizing what was happening.

"You!" The Editor said, pointing at Guard 107. "Please read the term that's repeatedly highlighted."

The guard leaned in as he skimmed the page, and said, "The Jew."

"Very good," The Editor said. "That's not the kind of term a compassionate person, like Charles, would ever say."

Dickens broke in with, "But that's not the full story. I later admitted I had been insensitive with my …"

The Editor interrupted with, "It doesn't matter, does it?"

"It matters to me," Dickens said.

The Editor chuckled, and said, "What matters to you is definitely not important. I've got a whole stack of letters here when you displayed your insensitivity, along with several other examples of how you leaned on stereotypes in your books."

"I never meant any harm," Dickens said. "And I listened to the complaints, and made changes to my books …"

"What?" The Editor asked, interrupting with a smile. "Are you admitting that you went back and revised your own book after you learned you had been wrong?"

Dickens looked away, having to admit The Editor had made a good point.

"Revising books to reflect new information," The Editor said. "Sounds like you really do understand the Modern Truth Movement."

Dickens was fuming now. He couldn't speak.

"What's wrong, Charles?" The Editor asked. "Why did you get so quiet?"

Dickens knew his actions were much different than the Modern Truth Movement, but his rage, and his mental cloudiness, hindered him from being able to defend himself.

"What if I," The Editor said, "did to you what Nietzsche's sister did to him?"

Dickens looked at The Editor, terrified.

"Your use of stereotypes would make more extreme ideas seem plausible," The Editor said, holding up the stack of letters. "But what if I presented to the world Charles Dickens' secret manifesto? Something he wanted released upon his death, but was so dark his loving family never released it, knowing how badly it would tarnish his legacy."

The Overseer, having an epiphany, added, "Couldn't we just use Nietzsche's sister's text, and say Dickens was the real author?

"That is a wonderful idea," The Editor said, with delight. "We could even say that Charles and Friedrich wrote the book together, and then blamed everything on Elizabeth."

"Yeah!" The Overseer said, excited.

"Everyone will believe it," The Editor said. "No one will even bother to look up whether Charles and Friedrich could have known one another."

The Overseer nodded along.

"You really are a chip off the old block," The Editor said, giving The Overseer a side-hug and a loving kiss on the forehead. "I try to keep it to myself that this is my first-born son, but right now, my pride is too strong to keep it to myself."

The guards all exchanged glances with each other, revealing this was also news to them. Dickens looked at The Doctor, who seemed more annoyed than shocked by this revelation.

"In fact," The Editor said. "This brings me to my next point."

He took a step toward the wall, and began addressing the entire room, saying, "I'm leaving for a few weeks. My son will be in charge. He's the only person I completely trust to run this operation."

"Tell them what you're doing, dad," The Overseer said.

The Editor chuckled and said, "I'm going to a remote region of Papua New Guinea. It's so remote it's impossible to get internet or even cell service. No phones. No televisions. Isn't that sad?"

Everyone in the room except Nietzsche and Dickens nodded in agreement.

"These poor people have never heard the gospel of prosperity," The Editor said, with a compassionate tone. "Their sinful ways have led them to great poverty, and hopefully, if God anoints me enough, I will convert them to our ways. And, since this region is one of the finest on Earth for growing coffee, they stand to make a lot of money as Christ-centered capitalists. Before long, they'll have cell service, broadband, and a Chick-Fil-A in every village."

"Amen," the room said collectively.

"Amen," The Editor repeated. "Since I'll be unreachable, I am placing my son in charge. Completely in charge. Up to, and including, the Kill Switch."

The Doctor seemed like he wanted to dispute these directions, but he moved back against the wall, saying nothing.

"I trust him completely," The Editor said. "Take his orders as you would my own."

"And as for you, Charles and Friedrich," The Editor said. "You've heard my pitch. If you stop trying to fight us, and make the Revisions we want, your legacies will only improve. If you keep resisting, we will make sure you both are remembered as history's greatest monsters."

He walked over and put his arm around his son, and said, "But my son has a gift I do not have. He can be very persuasive."

He kissed his son on the forehead again, and said, "I've asked him to use his God-given gifts in any way he sees fit."

With his smile still as wide as ever, The Editor gave exaggerated waves goodbye and left the room, with an air of pride after having delivered such a powerful sermon.

The Doctor, who looked relaxed now that The Editor was gone, said, "I'm glad your daddy finally gave you permission to do something."

"Shut up, doctor!" The Overseer said, with a sarcastic emphasis on "doctor."

"Did you know he was The Editor's son?" Dickens asked The Doctor.

"Yes," The Doctor said. "I was told to keep it a secret, since he's the son who disgraced the family."

"How did he disgrace the family?" Nietzsche asked.

"Oh," The Overseer said. "I'm the disgraced one? Doctor?"

"I am a doctor!" The Doctor yelled.

"You have an honorary doctorate in theology," The Overseer yelled. "And you'd still be a preacher if you hadn't …"

"Stop!" The Doctor yelled.

"Fine!" The Overseer said, to The Doctor. "But this isn't finished."

"Fine!" The Doctor said, resuming his position against the wall, pouting like a child.

"So, that's what this place is?" Nietzsche asked. "A place to send the people who embarrassed The Editor?"

"That's what it sounds like to me," Dickens said, turning to the guards. "Is that why you all are here, too?"

"Stop!" The Overseer yelled, interrupting. "That's enough. I'm not going to give you every detail about our operation."

"But you must have done something really bad?" Nietzsche said.

"Worse than you could imagine," The Doctor added.

"What did he do?" Dickens asked.

"Oh," The Doctor said, "I don't even know where to begin."

The Overseer walked over and slapped The Doctor on the back of the head, causing him to lose balance and stumble into the wall.

"You idiot!" The Overseer yell to The Doctor. "Can't you see what they're doing?"

The Doctor gave a look of defiance but remained quiet.

"They want us to show our weaknesses, so they can exploit them," The Overseer said. "And you are playing right into their hands."

They held a long look, and then The Doctor nodded.

"Not another word," The Overseer said to The Doctor, before turning his attention back to Dickens. "I will tell you one little detail. Neither me nor The Doctor have anything left to lose on this Earth. The purpose of both of our lives is about doing good works so we can make it to heaven."

Dickens could now see the similarities between The Overseer and The Editor, especially when they were grandstanding.

"We both trust that my father knows God's word, and knows how to hear God's voice," The Overseer said. "We both work to complete his mission here on earth, and THAT is what we are doing here at the CRC."

The Doctor nodded.

"Having nothing to lose comes with its advantages," The Overseer said, followed by a pause for emphasis. "It frees you up to do whatever is necessary."

The Overseer motioned to Guard 93, who nodded and ran out.

Dickens and Nietzsche looked at one another briefly but then looked away.

"Mr. Dickens, unlike your nihilist pal," The Overseer said, emulating his father's method of speaking. "I think you have something to offer."

The Overseer walked over and patted Nietzsche on the head, condescendingly, and said, "My father screwed up when he had you Resurrected. You've been nothing but a hassle, and your books were never worth Revising."

The head-patting grew more intense, before he hauled back and smacked Nietzsche across the face. Nietzsche buckled to the ground and, since his hands were still cuffed behind his back, hit the ground hard. The Overseer stood over Nietzsche like a victorious boxer.

"I have no interest in seeing you Revise your worthless books," The Overseer said, with a mischievous grin. "But, since you're here, I did think of a way you might be of use."

Guard 93 ran back in, holding one side of the double-doors open, and motioning for another guard to hold open the other side. Outside the doors, a sound of clickity-clacking steps grew louder and louder until two men, who looked like policemen wearing cowboy hats, led in a large brown horse. When the horse's smell wafted toward Dickens, he felt another pang of loss for his Birth Life.

The policemen walked the horse up toward The Overseer, who gave it a side-mouthed "click click click" sound, as stroked its mane.

"Mr. Dickens, did you know your pal was a great lover of animals?" The Overseer said, while gazing affectionately at the horse. "He couldn't stand watching them harmed in any way."

Dickens didn't respond.

"You said you weren't Revising another word, and there was nothing we could do to convince you," The Overseer said. "What I would like to know, is if we can get ole Friedrich here to convince you."

The Overseer stepped back from the horse, and then nodded at Guard 84. The guard removed his nightstick from his belt, and began slapping it into the palm of his hand, as he slowly walked toward the horse.

Dickens locked eyes with Nietzsche, whose face was filled with sheer terror.

"I know you want to return to Revising, Mr. Dickens," The Overseer said. "Whenever you're ready to start, I'll make this stop.

Dickens had witnessed horrible sights in his life, and he had seen first-hand the effect horrible episodes have on those who suffer them. But still, he could see this experience would be next-level horror for Nietzsche.

The Overseer had his eyes locked on Dickens, whose eyes were on Nietzsche. Guard 83 stepped up to the trusting horse, raising his nightstick.

"Fine!" Dickens said. "I'm ready to start."

The Overseer held up his hand to stop the guard. Everyone froze for a moment.

"I must admit," The Overseer said, walking up to Dickens. "I'm a little disappointed."

The Overseer nodded to Guard 93, who escorted the two men and the horse out of the Resurrection Room.

The Overseer gave Dickens a long look he couldn't quite interpret, mostly since his look was always a little slack jawed, but he then looked at Guard 84, who shrugged and walked away. Dickens looked back over to Nietzsche who was still visibly shaking, but his relief the horse would not be tortured was unmistakable.

"You win," Dickens said to The Overseer. "Take me back to the Revision Room."

"Very well, Mr. Dickens" the Overseer said, exhaling. "Let's get you back to work."

Six guards swarmed Dickens, untied his arms and legs, and carried him out of the room, down a long corridor leading into the Revision Room. Dickens' body was forced into a seated position while he was still being held in the air. They lowered him onto a chair in front of his desk.

They restrained him across his torso with chains attached to the chair. The guards took those chains, wrapped them around his legs, and his upper arms, and looped them through a set of chains already attached to his desk. The rest of the guards let go of Dickens, as one of them pushed him up close enough to reach his keyboard. The guards fanned out into a C-shaped formation around his desk.

The Overseer pushed his way between two guards, approaching Dickens' chair.

"Mr. Dickens, you are a much bigger fool than I anticipated," The Overseer said, leaning in with his mouth directly in the writer's ear. "You just taught us how to manipulate you into working. I could have Mr. Nietzsche, and a whole parade of horses, marched in here to torture."

The Overseer took a step back, saying to the guards, "If he even stops typing, break one of his knee caps. You got it?"

The guards all nodded.

"Good," The Overseer said, as he walked back over to his desk, sat down, kicked his legs up, and kept his gaze zeroed in on Dickens.

Dickens knew there was nothing he could do, so he scrambled to put himself back in Scrooge's frame of mind. With his body weighted down with chains, and his hands uncomfortably suspended above the keyboard, he began typing.

CHAPTER 4: THE LAST OF THE SPIRITS

or

He stopped typing. He'd been having so much fun coming up with alternative chapter titles, but now it seemed stupid. He couldn't win, and there was no point trying. But he at least needed to be consistent. As he contemplated, Guard 93, began tapping Dickens' kneecap with his nightstick, in a not-so-subtle threat.

He typed out the only alternative title he could think of:

I'M NOT IN THE MOOD FOR FUNNY TITLES ANYMORE

He moved on to depicting The Ghost of Christmas Future.

***

The final ghost, The Ghost of Christmas Future, floated toward me without making a sound. Knowing the drill by now, I involuntarily bent down on one knee. The Ghost was enveloped in a black robe, which hid its head, its limbs, and in fact, its entire form, except for one long, bony, outstretched hand.

"Are you the Ghost of Christmas Future?" I asked, even though it was obvious.

It didn't answer, but pointed with a long, skeletal finger.

"I assume you aim to reveal things to me that have yet to happen," I asked, my voice trembling. "Is that so?"

The Ghost, again, didn't answer. I suppose it was another obvious question.

"Lead on," I said. "The night is fading fast."

The Ghost floated in a direction, and I followed.

We didn't so much enter the city, but rather, the city sprang up around us. Abruptly, it was daytime, and we were in the heart of it — at the London Stock Exchange, amongst the merchants; who hurried up and down, clanked the money in their pockets, looked at their watches, and talked in groups like teenage cliques.

I'd been there many times, and I recognized numerous faces.

The Ghost stopped by a cluster of businessmen, and extended his willowy hand. I obeyed by sidling up to eavesdrop on their conversation.

"I haven't heard anything," said a fat man with an enormous chin. "All I know is he's dead."

"Was he sick or something?" another man asked, taking a lump of tobacco out of a pouch to fill his pipe. "I thought he'd never die."

"I'm more concerned about the final resting place of his money," said a red-faced gentleman with a long turkey neck.

"All I know is he didn't leave it to me," said the large-chinned man, yawning.

This comment was received with a general laugh.

"It's likely to be a cheap funeral," the chin man said. "I can't think of a single person who would WANT to go."

"I'd go if lunch is provided," said a man who had yet to chime in, who was the fattest of them all. "If there's no food, though, I'll have to celebrate … um, I mean mourn … privately."

Another hearty laugh from the group.

"Well, I am the most disinterested among you, after all," said the first speaker, "this conversation has lasted longer than any I ever had with him."

***

Dickens glanced down at The Editor's notes, which he remembered included a suggestion for this scene.

"You should make it clear in this scene that Scrooge was a good man of business. You should add in a little dialogue about the respect they have for him in business. Otherwise these men could be seen as fitting the unfair stereotype that wealthy people are heartless."

Dickens cringed as he read this suggestion. But he saw no other choice.

***

"Gentlemen," said a man standing close to the group. "You all know he, at times, was a difficult person to be around. But do you easily forget what he taught us about money management? In fact, some of you wouldn't have two coins to rub together if it wasn't for his sound advice. You should be ashamed of yourselves."

The men stood and looked at one another with guilt and shame. Suddenly they all broke into tears, at the loss of their financial mentor.

***

Dickens involuntarily rolled his eyes at the dialogue he'd just written.

***

The Ghost and I moved out of the busy scene and into an obscure part of town. The streets were narrow and dirty; the shops and houses dilapidated; the people drunken, sloppy, ugly.

The alleys spewed their stench, and filth, and soot upon the meandering streets; and the whole area reeked of crime, with grime, and despair.

Deep in the bowels of this cesspool, we came upon a shop that looked more like the dwelling of a hoarder than a place of business. Among the piles of discarded wares, by a charcoal stove, was a grey-haired rascal, Old Joe.

A woman ran in with a heavy bundle slung over her shoulder. From another corner of the room, another woman entered with a similar bundle, and from another direction came a man with a bundle of his own. They all looked at one another with shock, which turned into roars of laughter.

"Well, three customers at once," Old Joe said. "That can mean only one thing, and I hope it wasn't a friend of mine."

"Don't worry, Joe," the first woman said. "He was no one's friend."

The man who had entered the store last elected to show his loot first. It wasn't very impressive. A pencil-case, a pair of cufflinks, and a damaged pocket watch. Joe carefully examined the items and, upon the wall, chalked up the sum he'd be willing to pay.

Next, the second woman's bundle was composed of sheets, towels, and a pair of sugar-tongs. Joe chalked up her price on the wall as well.

"And now undo my bundle, Joe," said the first woman.

Joe went down on his knees to open it, and after untying a ludicrous number of knots, dragged out a roll of dark material.

"What is this?" Old Joe asked. "Bed curtains?"

"Ah," the woman said. "Bed curtains."

"You took them down, rings and all, with him lying there?" Joe asked, amused.

"I did," cried the woman. "Why not?"

The woman, who perhaps should have felt some sense of shame, rather beamed with pride.

***

Dickens read over The Editor's note on this scene, and he could hardly believe it. Could it be possible to think this was actually a good idea? Oh, well, he thought, preparing to type. Here it goes!

***

"Spirit," I said. "You have shown me a den of thieves, who yes, are terrible people. But I do believe both of us know, these thieves would not have had to steal, if the government would have just cut taxes, for if they had, the dead man's wealth would have trickled down to them. Instead, they had to steal the man's wealth, forcing their share to trickle down. Oh, the suffering taxes causes for all of us! And these poor people are no exception."

***

Dickens couldn't help but wonder why The Editor wanted Cratchit to be blamed for his own financial struggles, but, the thieves, were somehow portrayed as victims of high taxes. Good poor people deserve it, but bad poor people don't? Why?

He dismissed this question quickly, though. It would never make sense to him. He forced himself to keep typing.

***

"Spirit," I said, shaking from head to foot. "Why do you continue torturing me?"

Just when I thought I could stand no more, the scene changed, and we were standing by a bare, uncurtained bed. A pale light rose out of thin air and fell straight upon the bed. And on it was the plundered, unwatched, unmourned, uncared for body of a man covered with a thin bedsheet.

My mind raced with thoughts about this man. If this man could be raised up now, what would be his first thoughts? Would it be the trivial nonsense that so frequently occupied a man's mind, or would his perspective have changed? Changes of mind and changes of action?

***

Dickens chuckled to himself, which was surprising, since he didn't think it was possible to chuckle under these circumstances. But the above section struck him as ironic, almost prophetic, that he had dwelt on the idea of the mysterious man in the bed being raised from the dead and how such an act would have changed the man's perspective on life. It was a phrase that, in that moment, he couldn't even remember writing. But it amused him that it was there, since he now knew exactly what a "raised up" man's thoughts would be.

This feeling didn't last long, though, as a stern look from The Overseer erased the moment of non-suffering. He went back to typing.

***

"Let me see SYMPATHY from a death," I said to the Ghost, pleading.

With another wave of the Ghost's robe, I found myself back inside the home of Bob Cratchit. The mother and most of her children were seated around the fire. Not a sound was made by mother or child. The mother was sewing, and the room was so quiet the sound of the needles rang in my ears.

Bob walked in, and she quickly sat down her sewing and hurried to meet him. His tea was ready for him on the stove, and she, as well as all the children, tried to help him get to his tea faster. When he sat down, the two youngest Cratchits got upon his knees and laid, each child with a little cheek against his face.

"You went today?" the wife asked.

"I did," returned Bob. "I promised him I would visit on Sundays."

Bob's voice choked off the sentence, as his face contorted with sorrow. The children all rushed to offer Bob comfort, which appeared bitter-sweet for him, as he appreciated the desire to ease his pain, but the pain he felt was severe.

"My dears," Bob said once he had half-composed himself. "Let us never forget the example he set for all of us; how patient and how mild he was; let it always bring us closer together, the memory of our big-hearted, but Tiny, Tim."

"Tiny Tim?" I yelled at the Ghost. "For fuck sake, did I really have to specify the PERSON for whom I wished to see sympathy?"

***

This line amused Dickens, but his amusement evaporated once he looked down at a note from The Editor concerning this scene.

"It should be clear Tiny Tim's illness was either due to some sinful behavior the child had engaged in, or due to God's judgement upon Bob. And for the love of Pete, don't say anything that will make people think children deserve government-provided health care. Such a thing could ruin this entire Modern Truth Movement."

Dickens wasn't thinking straight. The fogginess in his mind was growing denser and denser. He had no idea how provoking sympathy for a terminally-ill child would ruin the Modern Truth Movement. He couldn't tell if the note really made no sense, or whether he was too exhausted to understand.

He decided to play it safe and write in The Editor's suggestions.

***

Bob continued speaking to his children, saying, "But no matter how much this hurts, we must keep in mind that I am a faithless man. I'm sure you children all know my lack of wealth is completely linked to my sinful ways, right?"

Phrases like "well, sure," and "of course," and "we know," came to all of the children's mouths without hesitation.

"But what you might not know," Bob said, "is Tiny Tim's illness, too, is linked to my heathen, freeloading lifestyle."

The children all nodded. Apparently, they already knew.

"Learn from my mistakes, children," Bob said. "Go to church. Pray. It will not only bring you abundant wealth, but you will also have children with virtually zero health problems."

Bob burst into tears and said, "Promise me you won't let this happen to my grandchildren."

The children all gave him solemn nods of agreement.

***

Dickens wasn't even really repulsed anymore. He was too beat down mentally and emotionally to care.

***

"*Ghost," I said. "I know we will soon part ways. Before we do, tell me the name of the man who we saw lying dead?"*

***

Dickens only got through that sentence before he stopped again. He was confused, once again, but this time it was about something he'd written himself.

"Why is Scrooge still asking who the dead guy was?" Dickens thought to himself. "Isn't it obvious? What was I thinking when I wrote this?"

He didn't have the motivation to figure it out, nor did he care enough to try. He decided to cross out the phrase and move on:

***

~~"*Ghost," I said. "I know we will soon part ways. Before we do, tell me the name of the man who we saw lying dead?"*~~

I accompanied the Ghost down zigzagging streets until we came upon an iron gate. He paused, looked both ways, and went through the gate, which led to a churchyard.

The Ghost guided me past rows of headstones and stopped before one overrun by grass and weeds. The plot was covered, from neglect, by vegetation's death, not life. The Ghost pointed down at the grave, and I took a step toward it. I read the name etched on the front of the neglected grave: Ebenezer Scrooge.

"Spirit." I cried. "I will never be the same man I was before the three ghosts visited me."

For the first time The Ghost's hand appeared to shake.

"I will keep Christmas in my heart all year," I cried. "I'll never spell Christmas with an 'X', and I vow to always be a valiant soldier in the War on Christmas."

Out of desperation, I fell to my knees to beg, as I saw the Ghost's hood and dress begin to shrink, and dissipate, into thin air.

CHAPTER 5: THE END OF IT
or
THIS STORY NO LONGER MAKES ANY FUCKING SENSE

I was back at home. In my bedroom. The bedpost was mine. The bed was mine. The room was mine. Most importantly, the time before me was mine, allowing me to make amends.

I climbed out of bed and fell to my knees, "Jacob Marley, you have saved me from myself. You have managed to help a man still on this earth."

***

Dickens stopped typing, and thought, "Help him with what? This ending makes no sense at all anymore."

His apathy, which was clearly showing in his Revising now, was still strong, but he was still a writer, and careless writing mistakes gnawed at him.

"If he's a revered businessman," Dickens asked himself, "who is rich because his life is not full of sin, what is his lesson learned? Is he being punished for not being nice? He's not punished for THAT either?"

Dickens perceived with his peripheral vision a look of displeasure from The Overseer, so he knew he at least needed to look busy. He decided to look through the last of The Editor's notes to see if there were any clues to his desired ending.

"In the final scene," The Editor wrote, "on Christmas morning, this would be a perfect place for Scrooge to get saved. Cut out the part about him buying the goose and giving it to Bob Cratchit. Instead, he could go out on the street, eager to celebrate Christmas, and bump into a preacher who shares the gospel. Scrooge could get saved on Christmas morning. That would be the …"

He couldn't force himself to read the rest of that note, so he skimmed past it, moving on to notes at the very end.

"All you do is write 'to Tiny Tim, who did not die.'" The Editor wrote. "Shouldn't you say something else? It's a big part of the story, and this phrase feels like it was tossed in as an afterthought."

"Hmmmm," Dickens thought to himself. "Did The Editor just make a valid critique?"

Dickens couldn't tell. He was so tired he didn't trust his own opinion. Based on The Editor's previous notes, he didn't seem capable of suggesting a helpful change. Dickens decided to see if the next note made sense, knowing that for him to perceive two of The Editor's notes as valid, would mean he was certainly too tired to think straight.

"In the last paragraph of the book," The Editor wrote, "you say 'He had no further intercourse with spirits.' Is it implied that Scrooge had sex with the ghosts? …"

Dickens had to stifle a laugh. He was tired, but not too tired to distinguish between a decent comment, and a staggeringly stupid one. This made him feel a little better.

"… A sex scene must have been in one of your first drafts," The Editor wrote. "You, wisely, cut it out. Did you forget to remove this line? I believe I'm right about this, because I see the next line is 'but lived upon the Total

Abstinence Principle', which is an obvious reference to him abstaining from sexual immorality. Saying he is abstinent, since he isn't married, is a very positive comment, but I would like to, altogether, avoid any references to ghost sex."

Dickens was dumbfounded. It would be reasonable for a modern person to not understand his little temperance joke, conflating ghostly "spirits" with alcoholic "spirits," but to jump to the conclusion of ghost sex, said a lot about The Editor's mind.

He looked at the very last of The Editor's notes, which wrote, "Ending the book with 'God bless us, everyone!' was fine for your Birth Life edition, but it doesn't really work with the Revision. I'm thinking you could have Tiny Tim shout, 'I declare the War on Christmas, is won!'"

Dickens was once again doubting himself. Not because this last note sounded valid, but rather it seemed too stupid even for The Editor. His eyesight was beginning to transform from blurry to double-vision, and he thought he must have read it wrong. Regardless, it was clear he couldn't go on like this. If he was ever going to finish this Revision, he would have to get some sleep.

Dickens rattled his chains to get the attention of The Overseer, whom he could see was maintaining the same laser-focus glare ever since they got back to the Revision Room.

The Overseer slowly stood up and walked over to Dickens' desk, giving a quick "What do you want?" shrug.

"Sir," Dickens said, with a slight slur of speech, due to tiredness. "I understand the importance of this Revision, but I feel as if this will move along quicker if I could get a few hours of sleep."

"I'll do you an even bigger favor," The Overseer said, reaching into his back pocket, and turning to Guard 84. "Would you go grab me a bottle of water?"

The Overseer produced a flat, rounded can and removed its lid. The smell hit Dickens like a slap in the face, triggering a cringe from his first visit to America during his Birth Life. Something he found deeply disgusting about

Americans, and wished he'd never be forced to witness again: dipping smokeless tobacco.

The Overseer reached in the can, gathered a pinch, and slipped it between his lower lip and teeth, which made his lip bulge like someone who's just stepped out of the ring with a heavyweight boxer. He smiled at Dickens, revealing the sickening wad of tobacco, making him even queasier.

"Something you should know about this stuff," The Overseer said, as he gathered a much smaller pinch of tobacco from the can. "It'll give you a kick in the nuts like you've never felt."

The Overseer reached down and pulled back Dickens bottom lip, so tight he couldn't have broken free. He slipped the tobacco into Dickens' mouth, stepped back, and looked at Dickens, anticipating something, as if he'd just lit a firework with a rapidly burning fuse.

As Guard 84 returned with the bottle of water, The Overseer motioned to set it down on the desk, without ever breaking his gaze on Dickens.

Dickens felt his bottom lip beginning to burn, which, in a matter of seconds, escalated from tingling to scalding. He fought to keep it away from the top of his tongue, assuming it would taste disgusting, but as the tobacco juice mixed with his saliva, there was no use fighting it anymore. To his surprise, he found the taste somewhat agreeable.

Suddenly, his entire body filled with a rush of energy, unblurring his vision, and resuscitating his mind. The Overseer must have been able to see this transformation form on Dickens' face, as he smiled again like a giddy schoolboy.

"Okay," The Overseer said, grabbing Dickens' trashcan and holding it up to his chin. "Time to spit it out."

Dickens was a little confused, since it had only been in his mouth for 30 seconds, and, he was starting to enjoy it.

"Come on," The Overseer said. "Spit it out!"

Dickens obeyed and began spitting into the trashcan, which proved itself to be difficult, though, as straggling strings of tobacco were still stuck in his front lip.

"Open up," The Overseer said, raising the bottle of water, and tilting Dickens' head back. "You'll need to rinse the rest of that out."

Dickens allowed his mouth to fill up with water, swished it around, and spit it out.

"Since you're a dip newbie, you'd get sick if you'd kept it in much longer," The Overseer said, clearly proud of himself. "But you feel better, don't ya?"

"Yes," Dickens said, feeling energized. "Thank you."

"Good," The Overseer said. "I got a whole can of it. Next time you start feeling sleepy, just let me know."

Dickens nodded, as clarity swept into his mind like gale-force winds, clearing away the fog that plagued him since his Resurrection. He felt like his old self. His Birth-Life self. He'd forgotten how sharp and quick his mind had been.

"My dad's not a fan of me using this, but he's never tried it," The Overseer said. "It'll take you some time to get used to dippin', but, once you do, you'll think you've died and gone to heaven."

The Overseer patted Dickens on the back, turned, and walked back toward his desk.

An idea popped in Dickens head. The plan sounded perfect, but there was no time to think it over. It required him to act fast. Now!

"Oh," Dickens said. "I DID die and go to heaven!"

The Overseer turned around, shocked, and said, "What did you just say?"

Dickens gulped hard, not sure it this was a good idea, but there was no turning back.

"I DID die," he said, annunciating forcefully. "I DID go to heaven."

The Overseer turned and looked toward the guards, and said, "Am I crazy, or did he just say he went to heaven?"

"You are not crazy, sir," Guard 93 said, mouth agape. "That's what he said."

Turning to Dickens, The Overseer said, "My dad said no Revisers remember the afterlife."

"Well," Dickens said. "I remember."

"Why didn't you tell somebody?" he asked.

"No one asked," Dickens said, confidently, even though he was filled with uncertainty.

The Overseer stared at Dickens, sizing him up, and then turned to the guards.

"Go wake up The Doctor," The Overseer said to Guard 93. "Get 'em over here, now!"

Guard 93 trotted out of the room.

He leaned up against Dickens' desk, and with a look of suspicion and intrigue, he asked, "Tell me, what exactly do you remember?"

"I don't even know where to begin," Dickens said, smiling. "The streets of gold are lovely."

"You serious?" he asked, excitedly. "You've seen the streets of gold?"

"Oh, yes," he said, forming a look of awe. "I used to live there."

"You had a house on the streets of gold?" The Overseer asked, astonished.

"I wish," he said, woefully. "I was a vagrant."

"What?" he asked.

"I begged people for food," Dickens said, "and spare change."

"Oh, bullshit!" The Overseer said, skeptical. "There ain't no panhandlers in heaven."

"Bullshit?" he asked. "You don't believe in an afterlife?"

"No, no, no," The Overseer said, earnest. "You misunderstood me. I just always thought that …"

"With all due respect," Dickens said, interrupting. "Where in the bible does it say there are no panhandlers in heaven?"

Dickens maintained his confident tone, as he hoped there really wasn't anything in the bible about panhandling.

"Um, I don't know …" The Overseer said, turning to Guard 84. "Go see if you can figure out how to get a hold of my father."

"Go find somebody," The Overseer said to Guard 107. "Anybody who knows the bible backwards and forwards, and you ask them if the bible mentions panhandlers in heaven."

The guards ran off as The Overseer turned back to Dickens, and asked, "You are saying you went to heaven and chose to be a bum?"

"No!" Dickens said, commandingly. "It was my punishment."

"Oh, come on," he said. "He would have sent you to hell if you needed punishment."

"No," Dickens said, almost yelling. "I was NOT sent to hell. I did great works in my life. I wrote books that helped people. I not only showed empathy, I cultivated empathy in others. I depicted poor people as nobler than royalty. A biblical scholar like yourself surely knows how highly Jesus esteemed those trapped in the cycle of poverty."

The Overseer brushed off that comment, and asked, "So, why were you punished?"

"Because my heart was unclean," he said, now on a roll. "I was a man of great wealth. I loved money too much, which, as you know, the bible says is the root of all evil."

"Yes," The Overseer said, nodding enthusiastically. "But my dad always said that verse was misinterpreted."

"How so?" Dickens asked.

The Overseer looked toward the ceiling, contemplating, but finally said, "I can't remember."

"Well," Dickens said, "I can't speak with any authority on the bible, God's word. But I can tell you the words God told me at the pearly gates."

"Whoa!" The Overseer said, mesmerized.

"I was told that, despite my filthy, greedy heart," Dickens said, "my good works in life were deemed strong enough to earn an appointment to heaven. Heaven had mercy, but just enough to allow me to enter the gates. I received zero rewards beyond that."

"You serious?" he said.

"Of course," he said. "Why would anyone lie about such a thing?"

The Overseer nodded.

"I remember this one time, up in Heaven," Dickens said, his face lighting up, "when I saw this man I'd known in my life. A beggar. A kind man, but I passed him, every day, and gave him nothing. He would ask 'Do you have spare change?' and even though I always did have spare change, I'd go through this silly little routine where I'd pat my pockets, pretending as if I had nothing on me, and then I'd act forlorn, saying, 'Sorry. I never carry change in these trousers.'"

The Overseer appeared to also be a practitioner of the patting-pockets charade, as his face grew red with embarrassment.

"I saw him walking down the streets of gold, wearing the finest clothes I've ever seen," Dickens said, dramatically. "I was so desperate, I asked him the exact thing he used to ask me."

"What did he do?" The Overseer asked.

"What I didn't deserve," Dickens said, lowering his head with theatrically fake humility. "He didn't give me spare change. He gave me a bar of gold."

"Like, how big of a bar?" The overseer asked, ecstatic. "A couple ounces?"

"More like a pound," he said with a look of pride, which gave an impression of being proud of the bar of gold, but, truly, he was proud this scheme was working.

"Whoa!" The Overseer said, his eyes widening.

Guard 84 and Guard 107 suddenly burst into the Revision Room.

"Your father's plane took off a few minutes ago, and he'll be in the air for 18 hours," Guard 84 said. "He left his cell in his office at the church, but we might be able to get a message to him when he lands. If not, it might be weeks before we could get a message to him."

"Shit!" The Overseer said, pointing to Guard 107. "What did you find out?"

"I got a hold of a theology professor at Oral Roberts University," Guard 107 said, a little out of breath. "He said there is nothing in scripture about panhandlers in heaven."

"Well," The Overseer said, nodding his head. "This might change everything. We should shut down operation until my father returns."

The guards nodded, as Guard 93 ran in.

"Did you hear back from The Doctor?" The Overseer asked.

"He's on his way," Guard 93 said. "He said Resurrected people don't remember the afterlife."

"Friedrich remembers the afterlife, too!" Dickens said, his mind on fire now.

"You mean Nietzsche?" The Overseer said, rolling his eyes. "Bullshit! There's no way they'd let Nietzsche into heaven."

"I didn't say he went to heaven," Dickens said.

The Overseer and the guards exchanged looks of shock.

"How do you know?" The Overseer asked.

"Well," he said. "You know Nietzsche and I were scheming together, right?"

"Yeah?" The Overseer said. "So?"

"Well," Dickens said. "Our plans were much bigger than simply escaping."

He waved at Dickens in that circular, "keep talking" motion.

"The plan was to escape and get Nietzsche to a church, so he could get atonement for his sins," Dickens said. "He said no matter how bad this place was, it was infinitely better …."

Dickens trailed off, feigning sorrow.

"Wake up Nietzsche. Get him in here!" The Overseer yelled to the guards, all of whom ran off.

Dickens watched as The Overseer paced back and forth, noticeably in deep contemplation.

"How do I know you're telling the truth?" The Overseer asked. "What proof do you have?"

"I have no proof," Dickens said. "I understand why you wouldn't trust me, but, based on what Nietzsche told me, I wouldn't risk ANYTHING in this life. Even if you are 10 times more certain I am lying, it is not worth the risk. Especially for somebody who's done a lot of bad things in their life."

The Overseer nodded along, almost studiously.

The guards came in, dragging a very disheveled-looking Nietzsche into the Revision Room, and, while still holding his arms behind his back, pushed him up in front of The Overseer.

Nietzsche and The Overseer stared at each other for a moment.

"Sir," Dickens said. "May I continue Revising? I have a great idea for my next scene."

"No!" The Overseer said, turning toward Dickens. "The Revising might be done, if I get Mr. Nietzsche to confirm your story."

"I see, sir," Dickens said. "Can I at least write down a note. Just in case you choose to continue the Revising. I'm really bad about forgetting things if I don't …"

"Fine!" The Overseer yelled. "Take your stupid note!"

The Overseer motioned for the guards to turn Nietzsche around, so he and Dickens wouldn't be able to see one another.

"Mr. Nietzsche," The Overseer said, looking nervous. "I … uh … I am not exactly sure the best way to ask you this, but …"

Dickens started banging away on his keyboard, taking a note. On his computer screen the note stated, "Make sure Scrooge finds Jesus and then loves Christmas and make him …," but he frantically typed to the beat of the code Dickens and Nietzsche used in their bathrooms, tapping out the message, "u went 2 hell … u went 2 hell … u went 2 hell … u went 2 hell …"

"That's enough with the typing!" The Overseer said, maintaining his gaze at Nietzsche. "This is more important than your stupid note."

"Charles," Nietzsche said, with a shaky voice, "you told them?"

"I had to," Dickens said, still unable to see Nietzsche's face.

"Oh, Charles," Nietzsche yelled, whimpering. "They warned me not to tell."

The Overseer and the guards looked on with awe.

"I'm sorry," Dickens said, relieved Nietzsche had understood his message and curious what his friend would say next.

Letting out an even more painful-sounding whimper, Nietzsche said, "They will add another billion years to my punishment."

"What punishment?" The Overseer asked.

"No!" Nietzsche said. "I cannot say. I will burn!"

"Let them take you to a church," Dickens said. "Get atonement, as we planned all along."

"It is no use," Nietzsche said, crying. "HE told me there was no way to get saved once your Birth Life ends. I am doomed to hell. He told me!!"

"Who?" The Overseer asked. "Who told you that?"

"Who do you think?" Nietzsche said, followed by an enormous wail. "Jesus!"

The Overseer's look of curiosity instantly turned to that of horror. He motioned for the guards to let Nietzsche go.

"What are you talking about?" The Overseer said, grabbing Nietzsche by the lapels. "You talked to him. You heard his voice?"

"No," Nietzsche said. "He told it to me when...."

Nietzsche, perhaps emulating The Editor, held the dramatic pause, milking the suspense.

"… Jesus and I shared a jail cell last night," Nietzsche said, overcome with grief.

All of the color in the The Overseer's face faded to white, as he let go of Nietzsche.

To the guards, The Overseer asked, "Do any of you know what he's talking about?"

The guards shook their heads.

"You mean to tell me Jesus Christ is down in the holding tank of the Central Revision Complex?" The Overseer asked Nietzsche.

"He's gone now," Nietzsche said. "He said your father wanted to take him along on the trip. Something about delivering a Revised version of the Sermon on the Mount."

The Overseer nervously paced the floor.

"Oh, my God," The Overseer said, looking pale. "My father told me one time he wished the Sermon on the Mount could be rewritten, since it failed to mention punishment for the poor."

The guards all gasped.

"Did my father go too far?" The Overseer said, mostly to himself. Then, turning to the guards, more desperately asked. "Did my father go too far?"

The guards, clearly concerned themselves, shrugged back.

"What do I do?" The Overseer said, to no one in particular.

"Well, like I said," Dickens said, choosing his words carefully, "even if you think it's 10 times more likely he didn't, imagine your punishment if he did."

The Overseer began to pace back and forth, as everyone looked on, but suddenly, he stopped.

"Yeah," The Overseer said. "Fuck my father. I'm not going to hell for him."

The guards nodded, seemingly on board with the plan, too.

"I'm not just placing this operation on hold," The Overseer said, forcefully. "I'm shutting this entire thing down."

The guards appeared to be getting fired up about shutting down the operation, too.

"Follow me, and bring your guns," The Overseer said to the guards. "We're going to destroy the Resurrection Machine. Then, I'm flipping the Kill Switch."

"Hold on!" Nietzsche said. "As soon as you hit the Kill Switch, I'll be right back in hell. Could you at least allow me to spend my last few minutes on Earth unshackled?"

The Overseer looked back at Nietzsche, and, with a look of sympathy, turned to Guard 93 and nodded before running out of the room, followed by the other guards.

Guard 93 let Nietzsche out of his leg cuffs, and unlocked all of the restraints that had been placed on Dickens, and followed the other guards out of the room.

Nietzsche staggered over to his desk, rolled his chair over next to Dickens, and plopped down.

"Nicely done," Nietzsche said to Dickens. "I always assumed blind faith would be their undoing."

"I guess when you base your entire life on beliefs that defy logic, requiring zero evidence, you're pretty vulnerable to manipulation," Dickens said with a smile. "I saw an opportunity and went for it."

"Why didn't I think of that a long time ago?" Nietzsche said.

"Hey," Dickens said. "Your wailing about going back to hell was so believable. You should have been an actor."

Nietzsche chuckled, and said, "I'm confused why they didn't say, 'How could we Resurrect Jesus? He was already resurrected.'"

Dickens grinned and said, "How did you know The Editor had already considered revising the Sermon on the Mount?"

"I didn't," Nietzsche said. "But I'm not surprised."

"You didn't really spend the night in a jail cell with Jesus, did you?" Dickens asked.

Nietzsche gave a look of disappointment, "Charles, I warned you against drinking."

Dickens shrugged, feeling no shame about having used alcohol to help him cope with this dark time.

"Maybe that's how they'll amp up your punishment in hell," Dickens said. "Forcing you to drink."

"As long as I don't have to eat anymore KFC bowls," Nietzsche said, letting out a deep, cathartic laugh.

Dickens watched as Nietzsche gripped the side of the desk and staggered to his feet. He let out a long deep breath, while stretching out his legs and arms, and rubbing his wrist where he'd been cuffed. After popping his lower back, he ran over to The Overseer's desk, picked up the phone receiver, and pushed a few buttons.

"Code green," Nietzsche said, into the phone. "I repeat. Code green."

Nietzsche turned on The Overseer's computer. Confused, Dickens stood up and walked over. Once the computer woke up, Nietzsche opened up a window with a black background and white text, and began typing fast, expertly using all ten fingers.

"What are you doing?" Dickens asked.

"You'll see in a moment," Nietzsche said, as he continued typing.

Dickens shrugged, and asked, "So, once they hit the Kill Switch, we go back to death?"

"You will," Nietzsche said, as he stopped typing. "I won't."

"What?" Dickens asked.

***

The Overseer ran into the Resurrection Room with the cluster of guards. The lab techs sitting at their stations looked up, visibly puzzled.

"We're shutting this thing down," The Overseer said, pointing toward The Machine. "Do you all know how to do this, or do we need The Doctor?"

The lab techs looked at one another, not sure how to respond.

"What if we have the guards spray it with their guns?" The Overseer said. "Would that do the trick?"

One lab tech asked, "Is this some sort of joke?"

"This is no joke," The Overseer said. "I'm killing this tonight."

The Doctor appeared from around the corner, pushed a couple guards out of the way, running and shouting, "Nooooooo!"

The Doctor stood against The Machine with his arms stretched out, flattening his body and stretching to cover The Machine as much as possible.

"You're not killing this Machine," The Doctor said, almost crying. "If you do, it'll be over my dead body."

***

Before Nietzsche could respond to Dickens' question, Mark Twain walked in the room with his messenger bag over his shoulder. The Revision Room custodian, Custodian 8, walked in beside him.

"It should be ready for you," Nietzsche said, standing up and moving to the side.

"Good deal," Twain said, as he dropped onto the desk chair and began furiously typing.

Custodian 8 wandered over to Dickens' desk and grabbed the trash can which was filled with tobacco spit, but Nietzsche stopped him and said, "You don't have to do that anymore."

Dickens looked at Nietzsche, Twain, and Custodian 8, and said, "What is going on?"

Nietzsche placed his arm around Custodian 8, and with an American accent, said, "Mr. Dickens, allow me to introduce you to Mr. Friedrich Nietzsche."

"What?" Dickens asked. "You're an American?"

"I am," he said. "My name is Steve."

Dickens stood in confused silence.

Steve, which was apparently the faux Nietzsche's real name, pointed toward Twain, and said, "This guy over here is Mark. That really is his first name, but he's not Mark Twain. He's the Central Revision Complex's Information Technology specialist. He's the guy who actually designed that weird software that got you in trouble every day."

"Okay," Dickens said. "So, who are you?"

"I'm, an actor," Steve said. "Mark and I would be The Insiders."

"What?" Dickens said. "You're an actor?"

"Don't confuse me with that actor with the terrible British accent," Steve said. "But I am an actor who was hired to do that. Act like I'm a Reviser around other Revisers. To sniff out any plots to escape."

"You're on their side?" Dickens asked, getting angry.

"I WAS on their side," Steve explained, sternly. "After seeing what the Revisers went through, I just couldn't do it anymore. I sniffed out the Resistance, alright. But when I found them, I decided helping them was simply the right thing to do."

"I see," Dickens said, a little embarrassed that he'd been tricked, even though it was by a guy doing good things. "So, you made yourself a prisoner to help the Resistance?"

"Not exactly," Steve said, pointing with his thumb toward Mark. "We're sort of prisoners here, too. It's a long story ... and, frankly, it's pretty embarrassing."

Dickens remembered the discussion in the Resurrection Room about The Doctor and The Overseer both being disgraced. It was probably safe to assume Steve and Mark's stories were disgraceful too.

"Fair enough," Dickens said, looking over toward Mark, who was still typing furiously. "I won't pry."

"And Nietzsche, here," Steve said, pointing to the real Nietzsche, "He really was one of the first Revisers to be Resurrected. Mark and I, at first, didn't care either way about the Revising or any of that. But that changed when we saw how badly they treated Mr. Nietzsche."

Steve retrieved the fake mustache and wig from his desk and placed them on the real Nietzsche and suddenly, Dickens recognized it was really him. He remembered seeing photographs of the guy with the crazy mustache, only now he had a vacant look in his eyes.

"I still don't understand," Dickens asked. "Why did you start pretending to be Nietzsche?"

"Out of compassion," Steve said, "I had no plan at first, but it was the only way I could think of to get them to leave him alone."

"Why couldn't he stick up for himself?" Dickens asked.

"Nietzsche here had been a brilliant philosopher," Steve said, putting his arm around Nietzsche. "But for the final 11 years of his Birth Life, Nietzsche was insane. He couldn't talk. He could hardly do anything. That's the state he was Resurrected in. They would tell him to Revise his books, and he would just stare at them. They thought he was being stubborn. They started punishing him to get him to cooperate, which I just couldn't sit back and watch anymore."

Dickens nodded along.

"So," Steve said, "One day I decided to see if they could tell it was me if I put on his wig and mustache. No one knew a thing. I just sat there and pretended to be Nietzsche. I put him in a custodian's outfit, and he kind of wanders the building, taking out trash. He's also the one who put the alcohol in the rooms. That part's a long story and …"

"I got it," Mark yelled, suddenly stopping his typing. "Executing now."

***

"Does your father know about this?" The Doctor asked, body still strewn across The Machine.

"My father put me in charge," The Overseer said.

"Your father would never approve of this," The Doctor said.

"My father might not be the man I thought he was," he said. "I don't even know why he started doing this."

"Think about the future," The Doctor yelled. "Think about how much our children, and our children's children, will thank us for what we're doing."

"Oh, come on," The Overseer said. "Neither of us care about this movement. We just blindly followed along because my father told us to."

The Doctor pursed his lips together and exhaled slowly through his nostrils.

"Look," The Doctor said. "If you're having second thoughts about what we're doing, fine! But throwing away our future because of some small ethical dilemma, is frankly, insane!"

The Overseer lowered his head as The Doctor's words sank in. But then a painful smile formed across his face, like that of a man who just realized he'd been scammed. Epiphany, frustration, betrayal, resolve, all revealed in that tense smile.

"Insane?" The Overseer said, with a tense chuckle, still looking toward the ground.

"Yes!" The Doctor said, furious. "What you are suggesting is insane!"

The Overseer, slowly raised his head, and met The Doctor's eyes with a look that could have started a fire.

He said, "One of the most famous writers of all time, who we raised from the dead, just told me he went to heaven. One of the most famous philosophers of all time, who we also raised from the dead, just told me he went to hell. I just learned my father may have Resurrected Jesus Christ to force him to Revise the Sermon on the Mount."

"Why are you trusting …"

"All of this is being done to mislead the world, but without technically lying, in the hopes of destroying public education."

"It's for the greater good," The Doctor yelled.

"Good people don't do this kind of thing!" The Overseer said, to the others in the room. "We are not on the correct side of history. We are not even on the correct side of sanity."

No one in the room responded, but a few lowered their heads. Maybe out of fear. Maybe out of guilt.

"How am I just now seeing this?" The Overseer said, full of remorse. "My dad blackmailed both you and me, and we just went along, assuming he had our best interest at heart. No one with your best interests at heart, blackmails you."

The Doctor appeared to accept he wouldn't win this argument, taking a deep breath and slowly exhaling.

"Okay," The Doctor said, finally. "If you want to shut all of this down, it's your call. All I'm asking is for you to wait."

The Overseer ignored this, turning to the Resurrection Room techs, he asked, "Do any of you think you could operate this Machine?"

One of them nodded "yes" to The Overseer.

"You win," The Doctor said, with a greater urgency. "I get it. But it's late. None of us are thinking straight. Can we at least wait until morning so we can talk it over with clear heads?"

The Overseer continued to ignore The Doctor, saying to the tech who nodded, "Have you operated it before?"

The tech looked over to The Doctor, as if looking for guidance.

"Don't look at him," The Overseer yelled. "I'm the one asking you a question. Have you operated The Machine?"

"I have," the tech said, turning his attention back to The Overseer. With certainty but trepidation, he said, "I've operated The Machine on multiple occasions."

"I'll even tell your father I support your decision," The Doctor said, frantically. "All I ask is don't do anything rash."

The Overseer grabbed Guard 93's assault rifle, turned to The Doctor, raised the gun, and unloaded a round of bullets into The Doctor's chest.

***

Staring at the computer screen, Mark asked, "What should I do first?"

"Um," Steve said. "Other Resistance members first."

"Wake them up?" Mark asked.

"Yeah," Steve said. "Fire alarm. Just in their rooms. They'll know what to do."

Mark typed on his computer for a few seconds, and said, "Done."

"Revisions next?" Mark asked.

"Yeah," Steve said. "We should get that started."

"You got it," Mark said. "You should watch to make sure."

"We should let him do it," Steve said to Mark, pointing toward Dickens. "Charles, go over to your computer, open your manuscript, and tell us what you see."

Dickens nodded, sat down at his computer, which was still open to the manuscript.

"Okay," Dickens said, scrolling up and down the manuscript. "What am I looking for?"

"This!" Mark said, as he hit a button on his keyboard.

Dickens watched as the end of his manuscript began slowly disappearing, line by line, and was replaced with the original text. He smiled.

***

Everyone in the Resurrection Room was still in shock, having just watched The Doctor get shot and fall to the ground.

"Help me get him onto the table," The Overseer said to the guards. "We're going to restrain him, bring him back to life, and figure out how to shut this thing down with or without his help."

"Hey!" The Overseer said, again to the guards, who hadn't moved. "Now!"

"And you guys," The Overseer said to the other Resurrection Room techs. "Get going with whatever you have to do to get The Machine running."

The guards began hoisting The Doctor's body onto the table, and the still-stunned lab techs looked at one another, and slowly stood up to prep The Machine.

***

"The Revision virus seems to be running fine," Mark said. "It'll take a little time, but after it does, it would be impossible to use this software to Revise a single word."

Karl, Hemingway, and Shakespeare all came jogging through the Revision Room doors, wearing their pajamas. Before they could say anything to anyone, they noticed their computers were on, and slowly walked toward them, speechless, as they watched their Revisions being deleted and replaced with the original text.

"Okay," Mark said, to Steve. "I should probably see what I can do about The Machine."

"The Overseer and the guards ran out of here right before I called," Steve said. "They were going to go destroy The Machine themselves."

"Really?" Mark asked. "What happened?"

"I'll explain it later," Steve said.

Mark nodded, as he continued typing.

Steve looked over and saw all of the Revisers were still watching their Revisions disappear. Mesmerized. It was likely the only happy moment any of them had experienced in their Resurrection Lives.

"Uh," Mark said, looking up at Steve. "It's still online."

"Really?" Steve said, running around to look at the monitor. "It's operational?"

"That I can't tell," Mark said, with a hint of IT condescension. "But I think I can force The Machine's software to log out. Think I should do it?"

"Is Alex still down there?" Steve asked.

"Yep," Mark said. "But the holding cells down there are old-fashioned lock and key."

"No, I mean," Steve said. "Should we go see if Alex would know what to do?"

"Oh," Mark said. "Good thinking."

"I'm worried something went wrong," Steve said. "Maybe The Overseer had second thoughts."

Mark nodded in agreement while still looking at the screen.

"I'll go ahead and force The Machine to log out" Mark said. "Then I'll run down and grab Alex,"

Mark typed for a few seconds, and said, "Done!"

He hopped out of his chair and ran out of the Revision Room.

***

One of the Resurrection Room techs was stationed at The Machine's computer console, ready to type in specs for Resurrecting The Doctor, but, suddenly, the screen switched to a white screen with a black box in the middle, next to the words: "Password."

The lab tech's jaw dropped, and he quietly flailed his arms to get the attention of another tech who was prepping the table.

This tech's jaw dropped, too, when he saw the monitor.

The Overseer saw the techs gathering around The Machine, walked over, and asked, "What is it?"

"Ummmmmm," one of the techs said. "We don't know the password."

Stunned, The Overseer asked, "Are you serious?"

They all nodded.

"You don't know the password?" The Overseer asked. "You know how to run this thing, but you never learned the password?"

"That's correct," a tech said. "The Doctor showed us how to do everything, but he never shared the password."

Another tech said, "I've never seen it logged out."

"Can you guess it?" The Overseer asked.

"No," the same tech said. "It's one of those 13-letter passwords. It would take us forever to figure it out."

The Overseer began walking back and forth, frantically, saying "We've got to get him back to life. If not, I've committed murder."

The techs remained silent, unsure of how to respond.

"What about that IT guy?" The Overseer said. "Would he know it?

"No," a tech said. "The Doctor refused to even let Mark come in here."

"You are telling me," The Overseer said, "that the only person who can bring The Doctor back from the dead is The Doctor himself?"

"Yes," one of the techs said. "The only people, living or dead, would be The Doctor or Alex Wilderman."

"Great!" The Overseer said, lowering his head. "Dr. Wilderman's dead too."

"Sir," Guard 93 said, "that may not be entirely true."

***

Mark ran back into the Revision Room, and while gasping for air, said, "Alex is gone. Alex is gone!"

"Alex escaped?" Steve said.

"No," Mark said, still breathing heavily. "I got down there just as the guards were taking Alex upstairs."

"Why?" Steve asked.

"Only reason I can think of is they destroyed The Machine," Mark said, walking back to the desk. "And decided it was a mistake, so they are taking Alex up to fix it."

"Do we have time to let out all the Revisers in the Complex?" Steve asked.

"I'll unlock their doors right before I trip the exterior security system," Mark said. "But hopefully, they'll just die in their sleep when someone hits the Kill Switch."

"I guess that's the best we can do, since, if they don't hit the Kill Switch, we can't escape with 200 people," Steve said, pointing toward the members of The Resistance. "We'll have to take them with us."

"What?" Dickens said, breaking his attention from the manuscript changing. "We are going with you? What about the Kill Switch?"

Steve walked up to Dickens as the other Revisers gathered next to him, "It might even be better this way. You all are living proof of what's happened here."

"I understand that," Dickens said. "But I don't want a part in any of this. I just want to die."

"Me, too," Karl said.

"Me too," Shakespeare said.

Hemingway contemplated for a moment, and said, "Did marijuana ever become legal again?"

Steve and Mark both stared at Hemingway.

"What about absinthe?" Hemingway asked. "Also, Neech, what happened to your German accent?"

Steve didn't respond.

"Meh, fuck it!" Hemingway said, shrugging. "I want to die, too."

"Look, guys, I can appreciate that," Steve said. "But I don't see any choice. I thought they were going to hit the Kill Switch, but they didn't. We'll have to plan something else."

"We could dig at the back of our skulls," Dickens said, "And remove those microchips."

"I don't know what you're talking about," Steve said.

"And most importantly," Mark said. "We don't have time to talk about it. I'm about 90 seconds from taking down the security system to the outer doors of this place. We'll have a 3-minute window to get out."

Steve looked over at Mark, and then turned his attention back to Dickens, saying, "You really want to die that bad?"

"All I want in this life, is for it to end," Dickens said.

Steve looked toward the other Revisers, who nodded in agreement with Dickens.

"Fair enough," Steve said. "We'll get you out of here, and once we find a safe place, we'll look the other way while you all kill yourselves."

"Ugh!" Hemingway said, "Not again. I would like to die a different way this time."

"I'll kill you," Karl said. "I'll do it right now with my bare hands."

"Okay!" Hemingway said, oddly excited. "But I get to kill Shakespeare first."

"I would rather be eaten by fire ants," Shakespeare said. "I'd rather be baked into a pie!"

"Whatever!" Steve said. "I'll let you all figure that out, but we need to get out of here as soon as the security system is down."

***

The guards walked into the Resurrection Machine Room, escorting a disheveled-looking woman.

"Dr. Alex Wilderman," The Overseer said, smiling. "My father told me you died."

"I did," Alex said. "Your father killed me, and The Doctor Resurrected me, so I could be his tech support for The Machine."

"I'm sorry to hear that," The Overseer said. "Look, I am defying my father's plans, and I'm shutting down the entire Revision program."

Alex, still held by the guards, scanned the room, and said, "Your doctor looks like he needs The Machine."

"I had to kill him," The Overseer said. "He was trying to stop me from destroying The Machine. I would like your help to bring him back to life, and we'll just keep him tied up while we kill The Machine."

Alex gave The Overseer a puzzled look, "If I were to bring him back to life, he would just die again once I shut down The Machine."

"Why?" The Overseer asked.

"The Machine isn't just for bringing people back to life," Alex said. "That life is hopelessly dependent on the mechanisms built into the back of their skulls. Those mechanisms are programmed to shut off whenever it no longer detects signals transmitted from The Machine."

"I didn't know that," The Overseer said.

"I can tell you more about it if you'd like," Alex said.

The Overseer slowly lowered his head and said, "I'm a murderer. No matter what I do. Right?"

"I guess I don't know," Alex said. "Your intent was to kill him, but expecting to bring him back to life?"

"Yes!" The Overseer said.

"Murder was not your intent," Alex said, contemplating. "Intent is important."

The Overseer nodded.

"Say, for example," Alex said. "My intent with this Machine was to further humankind's understanding of our world. To move us past myths, or, I suppose, toward them, if the evidence proved them to be right. To help find justice for those who were killed, or who otherwise could provide testimony to serve justice. To provide much-needed insights into our history, in the hopes of it leading to a better future."

The Overseer nodded again, seeming more at peace.

"However," Alex said, "am I not, at least, in part to blame?"

The Overseer's peace began to fade.

"I introduced this Machine to the world," Alex said, "but I failed to question what harm it could bring. I've had a lot of time to think about this, downstairs, in my cell. Just because we can do something, doesn't mean we should. Just because good could come from something, doesn't mean the good outweighs the bad. I should have been more careful, and perhaps we could have stepped into the future, with fear and trembling, and eased it into the world …"

The Overseer was looking worse by the second, but it was unclear whether he, or anyone else in the room, was still listening to Alex.

Alex continued talking, "… I am grateful this is still the only prototype of The Machine on earth. Despite his intent, it does seem as if The Doctor succeeded at keeping this technology all to himself. Much better than me …"

The Overseer appeared to be on the edge of a severe breakdown, as Alex, still restrained by the guards, continued talking.

"… This man," Alex said, nodding toward The Doctor's body, "and others in the Modern Truth Movement, had much different intentions. So, if you look at the differences of intent, we can see an important moral difference, in one's heart, but, regardless of intent, when you consider the similar outcomes, of, say, me and the use of this Machine, and the outcomes of you shooting The Doctor …"

"Shut up!" The Overseer screamed. "Just let me think!"

Alex stopped talking for the first time in minutes. She didn't appear affected from the yelling at all, as if it was something that had happened to her all the time.

The Overseer walked over to the corner of the room, lowered his head and began mumbling something to himself. The guards, the lab techs, and Alex all looked at one another, confused about what was happening.

Suddenly, The Overseer raised his head, walked back to the center of the room, and said, "Okay. I've asked God for forgiveness. I should be good now."

"Good," Alex said. "I'm glad we got that settled. You still want me to kill The Machine?"

"Yes!" The Overseer said. "I'd like you to hit the Kill Switch, and, after that, destroy The Machine."

"I'm afraid to break it to you," Alex said. "But there is no Kill Switch."

***

Dickens sat in his desk chair and continued to watch his Revision delete itself, which he was happy to see, but he was already starting to feel lonely, even though he was in a room full of friendly people. He missed his family and friends during his Birth Life, and suspected, once he was no longer surrounded with the bizarre distractions of the Central Revision Complex, the pain and loneliness would grow even stronger.

For now, he sat and waited for word from Mark, who was still typing furiously, about when it was time to start running.

***

"Alex," The Overseer said. "What do you mean there is no Kill Switch?"

"I told your 'doctor'," she said, in a tone as if throwing air quotes around them, even though her hands were still restrained, "what I just told you. If The Machine is ever shut off, anybody who'd been brought back to life would die. And he said, 'like a kill switch?' and he just kept saying it. I think he just liked saying Kill Switch. I don't know. After a while he started acting as if I had said Kill Switch. He kept looking all over this thing for a switch. He would come downstairs and beg me to show him where the switch was. When, in reality, I never once told him there was a Kill Switch …"

"Okay!" The Overseer yelled. "I get it! Whatever! Just fry The Machine!"

The guards let go of Alex as she stepped up to the computer console on The Machine.

"I'm going to assume," Alex said, "That your doctor never updated the password."

She spoke, sarcastically, as she typed in, "1, 2, 3, 4, 5, 6, 7, 8, 9, 10, 11."

Sure enough, the log-in screen went away, Alex shook her head and laughed to herself.

"Wait!" The Overseer said.

He motioned to the guards, who grabbed Alex and moved her away from The Machine.

"I killed The Doctor with the intent to bring him back to life," The Overseer said, to the entire room. "My dad killed Alex and brought her back to life."

He began circling the room, addressing everyone, but no one in particular, as he mulled over this dilemma.

"My father has done evil with this Machine," he said. "I'm trying to stop it, but if I stop it, I kill Alex."

He began walking in faster circles.

"Do I get punished for that or does my dad?"

He was walking, and talking, even faster.

"Can I still get forgiveness if I'm not sure if I'm the one who sinned?"

He was walking, and talking, even faster.

"Also, I can say forgiveness for this, but then my dad ... what if he dies of malaria in New Guinea? I wouldn't be able to inform him he needed to ask forgiveness. Am I breaking the 'honor your father' commandment if I don't get a hold of him to make him aware of how circumstances have changed, and how he needs to ask forgiveness?"

He was walking, and talking, even faster.

"Is that even a thing? It's like I'm placing a barrier between my father and his ability to ask for forgiveness."

He was walking, and talking, even faster.

"It is all so confusing. Do you think I should call back that theology professor, so he can weigh in on this?"

"Your moral conundrum is all my fault," Alex said, loudly.

"Huh?" The Overseer said, as he stopped circling the room with his rapid-fire questions.

"My invention ushered everyone in this room into a completely different world," Alex said. "Your theologian can't provide quality insights, not from a book from the Bronze Age, or from any age, because the problem you're now facing is unique."

The Overseer nodded along thoughtfully.

"It's caused so much suffering," Alex said, sincerely. "I can't imagine an all-powerful, all-knowing God punishing you for destroying it."

"Wait!" The Overseer said, as if he just had a great idea. "When you were dead, do you remember anything from the afterlife?"

"I do," Alex said, smiling.

"I want you to tell me everything you remember about the afterlife," The Overseer said.

***

Mark said it would only take 90 seconds, but to Dickens, it felt as if an hour had passed. Maybe it had been only 60 seconds. Perhaps something had gone wrong, and it was taking longer than Mark had expected. Time is precise, Dickens thought. It's objective. The clock doesn't lie, but the length of time one feels, is highly subjective. The degree of suffering, perhaps?

His Resurrection Life had, in reality, only lasted a week, but it felt as long as his Birth Life. Even though, clearly, they were off by about 58 years. The suffering he'd endured already in his Resurrection Life had likely already outweighed that of his charmed, beautiful Birth Life.

Knowing this could make him an even stronger advocate for the poor, after The Revisers escaped. Despite his pleading, he was fairly certain that, as cruel as a Resurrection Life was, he would not opt for it to end, knowing of the suffering taking place in the modern world.

There was no point in resisting it. He didn't want this life, but now that he had it, dedicating it to help the less-fortunate, was simply the right thing to do.

***

"I'll do something even better," Alex said. "Let me SHOW you what I remember of the afterlife."

"What are you talking about?" The Overseer said.

"I have a simulation I can show you on The Machine," Alex said. "It's quite remarkable. It captures a very precise readout of what happens."

"Really?" The Overseer asked, excited. "How does it work?"

"It's hard to explain," Alex said. "It would be much easier for me to show you."

The Overseer nodded to the guards, who let her free. Alex walked back to the screen on The Machine and typed in a few commands. The Overseer walked up and looked over her shoulder.

"Where's the readout?" The Overseer asked, fascinated. "What does it say?"

"Give me just a moment," Alex said, still typing. "The screen will show you everything."

Alex typed in the last bit of code and hit enter, as the monitor on The Machine instantly went black. All lights on the power console went out. The Machine's hum stopped.

"What's going on?" The Overseer asked. "It looks like the thing just died."

Alex looked up at The Overseer with a smile, as she collapsed to her knees.

The guards caught her.

The Overseer turned to the lab techs and said, "What happened?"

One of the techs shrugged, and said, "She must have hit the Kill Switch."

"You bitch!" The Overseer said, kicking Alex in the stomach. "You said you were doing a simulation!"

Alex's face contorted in pain, but, briefly, reflected bliss, as she keeled over.

***

"Got it!" Mark yelled. "We have three minutes. Let's go!"

Mark and Steve took off down the Revision Room's main entrance. Dickens followed for two steps, when suddenly, the other Revisers, and the real Nietzsche, all collapsed to their knees. Dickens fell backward and grasped the walls of his cubicle to steady himself. His hearing went silent. His vision blurred.

Steve turned back and grabbed Dickens' lapels, pleading for something he couldn't hear. Mark grabbed Steve and pried loose his grip from Dickens' clothes. The two spun around, sprinting out of the Revision Room.

Dickens turned his head back toward the other Revisers, and watched as Hemingway, Shakespeare, Karl, and the real Nietzsche, all lay strung out across the Revision Room, like a war scene, convulsing, shaking, gasping for air, until they stopped moving.

Despite begging for death minutes earlier, Dickens' survival instincts kicked in. His heart raced. His body tensed. His face flushed. He could only take short, brisk breaths, worsened by a flood of emotions:

Jealousy, for The Insiders, Steve and Mark, rose within him. If things went well, they would receive recognition as heroes, and, although it seemed shallow, Dickens too desired recognition for his efforts at the Central Revision Complex. But, perhaps, justice would fail. What did justice even look like in this world? This led to:

Curiosity, about the modern world, filled his mind. He had seen, no doubt, an unfair representation of the world, and had no idea how normal people lived. What activities filled their days? What were key differences from his Birth Life? Was there a reason for digital clocks? Had he overestimated the importance of vending machines? Not knowing these answers was a:

Disappointment, for the loose ends, he would never see tied. Where did the real Nietzsche sleep at night? Did Steve sleep somewhere else in the complex? What did The Doctor, or The Overseer, do that was so disgraceful? Was his first Supervisor killed? Why did The Editor not even bring his cell phone on his trip? Why did both The Insiders have to dress up like Revisers? Had any women been Resurrected to Revise their books? Where did the vodka come from? Where did …

He stopped, overcome with:

Amusement, laughing at himself. This was real life, not one of his stories. He couldn't tie up all the loose ends. Answer all the nagging questions. Fill all the plot holes. He wanted to delay the ending, as he saw it approaching fast. Too fast. But we never get the ending that we want, do we?

He wasn't the creator of this universe. It was "The End," whether he liked it or not.

The flood of emotions stopped, as Dickens noticed his monitor. The Revision virus was complete, displaying the first page of his classic, timeless, and completely un-Revised novella, "A Christmas Carol." The most beautiful sight he had ever seen — in either of his lives.

Pain, like a sledgehammer to the chest, cracked Dickens out of euphoria. His head felt like it might implode. His stomach wrenched, like a thousand hangovers. Then, as suddenly as these symptoms appeared, they yielded to numbness.

His grip on the cubicle loosened, and, on instinct, he caught the edge of his desk. His hands were too weak. Sliding down the side of the desk, he gazed up at the computer screen, to take one last look at the first line of his book. He read the words:

"First of all, Marley was dead …"

The sight brought forth his last smile, as he collapsed to the floor, his mind fading to black.

THE END

Dear Reader,

Thank you so much for reading. I understand your time is valuable, and it means a lot for you to have chosen to spend any of that precious resource on my book. Hopefully, you found it time well spent. Please consider leaving a review on Amazon, so others considering my book will know whether it is worth their time, too.

If you have any questions or comments about the book, I would love to hear from you. Please feel free to email me: tedsatterfield@email.com.

More books are coming!

Thanks again,

Ted Satterfield